"Your arrogance is appalling."

Maggie drew a quivering breath. "And if you dare lay another hand on me..." She hesitated. "I'll make you sorry, that's all."

"I'm deeply repentant already," Jay said. "But you don't have to worry, Ms. Carlyle. Whether you believe it or not, I've never forced myself on a woman yet. I've never found it necessary. And you won't make me break that excellent rule."

He poured himself some more coffee, eyeing her meditatively. "Is it sex in general which turns you off, or the prospect of having it with me?"

"There's not the remotest possibility of that," Maggie snapped.

"Too true," he replied equably. "Unless I ask you. And I have no immediate plans to invite you to my bed."

SARA CRAVEN probably had the ideal upbringing for a budding writer. She grew up by the seaside in a house crammed with books, a box of old clothes to dress up in and a swing outside in a walled garden. She produced the opening of her first book at age five and is eternally grateful to her mother for having kept a straight face. Now she has more than twenty-five novels to her credit. The author is married and has two children.

Books by Sara Craven

HARLEQUIN PRESENTS

HARLEQUIN ROMANCE

SARA CRAVEN

storm force

Harlequin Books

TORONTO • NEW YORK • LONDON
AMSTERDAM • PARIS • SYDNEY • HAMBURG
STOCKHOLM • ATHENS • TOKYO • MILAN

Harlequin Presents first edition January 1991
ISBN 0-373-11330-7

Original hardcover edition published in 1989
by Mills & Boon Limited

CHAPTER ONE

'But, Maggie,' Philip Munroe's tone was plaintive, 'do you actually mean you're leaving me in the lurch?'

Maggie counted to ten under her breath. 'No, Philip,' she said courteously. 'I mean I'm taking some leave. A holiday that I've had booked for months, and which you've known all about for the same length of time.'

'But this is an emergency. Kylie St John is flying in tomorrow, and she'll want to know what we think about the new book.'

'The readers' reports and my detailed memorandum are on your desk, attached to the script.'

'I know that,' Philip said fretfully. 'I've seen them. They say that the whole middle section needs to be completely re-written.'

'They do indeed,' Maggie agreed cordially.

'But I can't tell her that. It's not the kind of news she wants to hear from me.'

Maggie smiled gently, pushing her red hair back from her forehead. 'Of course not. You have Maggie, the mad axe-woman, to do your dirty work with the authors, then you take them to lunch at the Connaught and kiss their egos better. It's a great system. Only I'm spending the next three weeks in Mauritius, and you'll have to wield the axe yourself for once.'

'But surely you could delay your flight for forty-eight hours. I'll get my secretary to ring the travel agent and...'

'I could do nothing of the sort,' Maggie said tersely. 'You seem to be overlooking the fact that I am not going to Mauritius alone.'

Philip stared at her. 'Oh, of course, you're going with Whatsit. I'd forgotten.'

'His name,' said Maggie, holding on to her temper with a superhuman effort, 'is Robin.'

'But I'm sure if matters were explained to him, he'd understand.'

'Why should he? I don't even understand myself.'

There was a loaded silence. Then Philip tried again. 'Kylie St John,' he began, 'is probably our most successful author.'

'She's also extremely temperamental, very tough, and a professional to her fingertips. Don't let her browbeat you,' Maggie advised, picking up her briefcase. 'Now, I'm going home to finish packing.'

'And is that your final word?'

Maggie groaned. 'Please don't sound so wounded,' she said. 'This is my first vacation in two and a half years.'

'Don't think I don't appreciate it,' Philip said warmly. 'No one's worked harder than you, darling, to put the firm on its feet. I've always been able to rely on you totally.'

'Good old Maggie—everybody's friend,' Maggie muttered.

'Well—if you want to put it that way.'

'No,' she said roundly. 'This is the way I want to put it, Philip. I am going on holiday with the man I love. You are going to deal with Kylie the Terrible. Call it your baptism of fire,' she added, as she swirled through the door, and down to her waiting cab.

Traffic was heavy, and she sat back in the corner of the taxi, looking out of the window with unseeing eyes.

It would do Philip no harm to stiffen his sinews and summon up the blood when dealing with some of the formidable ladies on their fiction list, she thought, defensively.

In any case, there was no way she was going to do anything to put her holiday in Mauritius in jeopardy. It had taken weeks of patient and subtle manoeuvring to get Robin to the stage of accepting the idea of a joint vacation anywhere.

She adored him, of course, but sometimes the old-fashioned principles rigorously instilled by his elderly mother were a little hard to take. And Robin loved her, she knew. There was a tacit agreement that—one day—they would be married. Perhaps the romantic surroundings of Mauritius would provide the spur he needed to make their engagement official, she thought wistfully. Especially if Mama wasn't around to ask why he needed to get married, when he was so comfortable at home with her...

Oh, don't be such a bitch, she adjured herself impatiently. Mrs Hervey can't be expected to look forward eagerly to losing her only son to another woman. She's come to depend on him, perhaps too much.

But I wish I could believe that, underneath, she likes me really, she added, with a little sigh.

She paid off the driver outside the block of flats where she lived, and dived up to the first floor.

Mrs Hervey would have every reason for disapproval if she could see the state of the flat, Maggie had to acknowledge as she dashed into the bedroom. It looked as if a bomb had hit it. She must have packed and unpacked her case at least half a dozen times. She had planned and looked forward to this holiday for such a long time, and bought loads of new clothes. So many, in fact, that they were almost like a trousseau, she thought, crossing her fingers surreptitiously. The problem was choosing the exact outfits to stir Robin to his very soul.

Well, it's decision time now, she told herself. You'll have to be at the airport in a few hours.

She was just rolling one of her new bikinis into a neat tube and stowing it into a corner of her case when the front door buzzer sounded.

She straightened, frowning. She wasn't expecting any callers. Surely Philip hadn't followed her home to make a last-ditch attempt to persuade her to change her mind?

'I'll kill him if so,' she muttered between clenched teeth.

'Yes?' she said curtly into the intercom.

'Vice Squad. Open up,' said her brother-in-law's familiar drawl.

'Sebastian?' she squealed, and opened the door. 'What are you doing here?'

'Hello, Ginger.' Sebastian Kirby bent and pecked her on the cheek. 'I phoned your office from the hotel, but they said you'd left for the day. Not ill, are you?'

'On the contrary, I'm going on holiday.'

'Really?' Sebastian's brows rose, and he looked frankly taken aback. 'Won't the hovel be a little bleak in October?'

'The cottage,' Maggie said with emphasis, 'is perfectly fine at any time of year. But, as it happens, I'm not going there for once. I'm heading for the sun. Mauritius, to be exact.'

'Going alone?' Sebastian followed her into the bedroom, and picked up another bikini, surveying it with a grin. 'Very—er, basic.'

'No.' Maggie's tone held a hint of challenge, as she snatched the tiny garment from him. 'I'm going with Robin.'

'Good lord!' Sebastian said blankly. 'You mean Mummy's actually let him off the leash at last?' He encountered Maggie's baleful look, and flung up his hands. 'OK. I'm sorry and it's none of my business. But neither Louie nor I can understand what you see in that stuffed shirt. However, if he makes you happy...'

'He does,' Maggie said levelly.

'Then have a wonderful holiday.' Sebastian sent her a placatory smile. 'Why don't I make us both some coffee?'

'Where is Louie? Why isn't she with you?' Maggie asked as he returned with a tray a few minutes later. 'She's all right, isn't she?' she added with sudden alarm. 'And the baby?'

'They're both blooming,' Sebastian reassured her. 'But we both felt it was better for her to stay in New York this time.' He grimaced slightly. 'I'm here on business, Mags, trouble-shooting for a major client. Don't tell me you haven't seen the headlines.'

'Headlines?' Maggie gave him a puzzled look as she took her beaker of coffee, then her brows snapped together in a thunderous frown. 'Oh, don't tell me you're here to rescue that bastard Jay Delaney.'

Sebastian perched on a corner of the dressing-table. 'That's a fairly harsh judgement.'

'Harsh?' Maggie echoed in disbelief. 'Oh, for pity's sake, Seb. He got drunk and raped a girl. You can't possibly be on his side.'

'I can and I am,' Sebastian told her levelly. 'He may have been accused of rape, admittedly, but that doesn't mean he's guilty. No charges have been brought yet.'

'Of course he's guilty,' Maggie said impatiently. 'It's perfectly obvious what happened. He's the big macho television star who's totally irresistible to women, and for once a girl tried to say no to him. And naturally his over-sized masculine ego couldn't take rejection. I hope he gets all that's coming to him.'

Sebastian stared at her. 'What's happened to the idea of someone being innocent until proved otherwise? Where's your womanly compassion?'

'I'm keeping that for his unfortunate victim.' Maggie wrestled to close the lid of her case. 'And if you're here to try to do a public relations whitewash job...'

'There'll be no whitewash,' Sebastian said quietly. 'Jay has agreed to "help the police with their enquiries", to use the classic phrase. I'm here to see that he's protected from the more virulent attacks of the gutter Press, that's all.'

'What a job,' Maggie said bitterly. 'Minder to an over-sexed yob, with a three-day growth and sprayed-on jeans.'

'For heaven's sake, Mags.' Sebastian looked shaken. 'I've never known you so bigoted—so vitriolic. You've never even met the guy. Have you ever watched his series?'

'Not if I can help it,' she said curtly. 'I don't belong to the school of thought which says that the world's problems can all be solved by an undercover agent with a gun in one hand and a woman in the other.' She gave a small angry laugh. 'He's probably started to believe his own publicity, and is convinced he's above the law in some godlike way. Or does he think because the fantasy girls in the series surrender to him that real women must as well?'

'We haven't exactly discussed that aspect of the situation,' said Sebastian. His expression was edgy, worried. 'Mags, I'm sure you're doing him an injustice. The girl who's accused him is a nightclub hostess—not exactly a defenceless schoolgirl.'

'Oh, I see.' Maggie jerkily fastened the straps of her case. 'And does her occupation give her no rights over her own body, or is anyone rich and famous allowed to use her as the whim takes them?'

'No, of course not.' Sebastian gave her a baffled glance. 'But doesn't it strike you as just a bit odd that she went to a newspaper to make her complaint, and not the police?'

'It's a man's world,' said Maggie bitterly. 'She probably knew when it was her word against Jay Delaney's that she wouldn't be believed.'

Sebastian sighed heavily. 'Ginger, I can't reason with you when you're like this. If you were to meet Jay—hear his side of things, you might...'

'He's the last person in the world I'd ever want to meet. I find men like Jay Delaney quite repulsive. And I'm glad that he's come across at least one girl who doesn't think he's God's gift, and is prepared to say so in public. I hope she says it in court.'

'No,' said Sebastian with sudden harshness. 'You prefer a mother's boy, don't you, Margaret? A wimp who has to travel half-way across the world to find the guts to go to bed with you.'

'Seb!' Maggie's cry held real distress.

He flushed deeply, and came across to her, patting her clumsily on the shoulder.

'Oh, lord, I didn't mean it Maggie. Forgive me. We shouldn't be quarrelling about this. I shouldn't have come here...'

'Of course you should,' she said quickly. 'I'd never have forgiven you if I'd found out you were in London and hadn't been to see me. We'll just have to agree to differ on the subject of Jay Delaney.' She paused. 'I'm only sorry I'm going away. We could have had a meal or something.'

'How long are you going to be in Mauritius?' Sebastian gave her a meditative glance.

'Three whole glorious weeks,' she sighed. 'Oh, I can't wait.'

'Well, you won't have to for much longer.' Sebastian forced a smile. 'I really hope it all works out for you, Ginger.' He dropped a light kiss on her hair. 'Now, I'll get out of the way, and leave you in peace. Look after yourself.'

'I always do,' she called after him.

Presently she heard her front door close and, collecting clean undies and the cool navy dress and jacket she was going to wear on the journey, she went into the bathroom.

She was disturbed by what had happened, she realised, as she lay in the warm water. She had adored Seb from the first moment Louie had introduced them, and they had never had anything approaching a cross word before.

Oh, damn Jay Delaney, she thought bitterly. Why couldn't he use some other PR company to represent him? And why does he have to be Seb's personal client? Someone like that doesn't deserve Seb's loyalty.

The story had broken first in one of the Sunday tabloids. Jay Delaney had given a party to mark the end of filming for his top-rated series, *McGuire*. It had started in a nightclub, and had moved back to the hotel where he had a suite. His victim, Debra Burrows, had worked at the nightclub and been invited to the party with some of the other hostesses.

On her own admission, Debbie had had too much to drink, and had gone into one of the other rooms to sleep it off. When she woke it was the early hours of the morning, and everyone else had left. She was alone with Jay Delaney, who had made it clear he expected to have sex with her, and when she refused he had raped her.

'I begged him to stop, but he wouldn't. He was like an animal,' she had told the newspaper. 'He said he could have any girl he wanted. That I should be flattered.

'I was such a fan of his. I worshipped him, and I was thrilled when he asked me to the party. But he's a sham, and a hypocrite. He's made me feel dirty—used.'

Her pretty bruised face staring from the front page had haunted Maggie ever since.

She thought, 'There but for the grace of God...'

Now, she drew a deep breath. She wouldn't spare Jay Delaney another thought, she vowed silently. He wasn't worth it, nor was any other man who preyed on women.

It was men like Robin who mattered. Men who were kind and tender—and decent.

Maggie stared at the dregs in her cup, asked herself if she wanted more coffee, and decided against it. She took another restive glance at her watch, and sighed.

Where was Robin? What on earth could have happened to him? He was supposed to have picked her up over half an hour ago, and he was usually punctual to a fault. She got up and began to prowl round the sitting-room, her uneasiness mounting. If traffic on the way to the airport was as heavy as it normally was, then they could end up by being extremely late. It was no good thinking they might be able to make up time on the journey either. Robin was a careful driver who didn't like to take chances.

All in all, the longed-for holiday wasn't getting off to a very good start. She had tried to telephone his home, but there had been no reply, signifying that he had set out at least.

Could the car have broken down, she wondered apprehensively, or, worse still, could there have been some kind of accident?

She shook herself. I won't think like that, she told herself determinedly. He's just been held up, that's all, but he'll be here in a minute, and until he arrives I'll do a last check—make sure I haven't forgotten anything.

She had just re-packed her handbag for the second time when she heard the buzzer.

'Oh, thank heavens.' She ran to answer the door. 'I was really beginning to worry,' she told him, smiling, and halted, her brows knotting. The first thing that occurred to her was that he was wearing a formal dark suit, the kind of thing he would put on for the office, instead of the casual slacks and shirt she would have expected. The second was that he looked pale and worried.

Her heart sank. Maybe her fears about an accident were only too justified.

'Come in.' She took his hand, drew him into the room. 'What's wrong? What's happened?'

He sat down on the sofa. He didn't look at her. 'Maggie, I can't go to Mauritius. I've had to cancel my flight.'

'Can't go?' she echoed incredulously. 'What do you mean? What are you talking about? We've been looking forward to it for months and...'

'I know, I know,' he cut in. 'And I feel terrible letting you down like this, but you see—it's Mother.'

For a moment, she looked at him blankly. She thought, I'm not hearing this. It cannot actually be happening, in nineteen-eighties Britain. This is some terrible joke.

Only, somehow, she didn't feel like laughing.

She moistened her lips with the tip of her tongue. She said quietly, 'I don't think I understand. Are you telling me your mother has imposed some kind of ban on your going—because if so, she's left it rather late in the day and...'

'Oh, no.' He looked horrified. 'It's nothing like that. She likes you, Maggie, she really does. No, she's been taken ill. The doctor thinks it may be her heart. She's had to go into hospital for tests. I went with her to see her settled in, and I've got to go back tonight.'

Maggie swallowed. 'Her heart?' she queried. 'But she's never had any problem before, has she? Isn't this rather sudden?'

Robin looked even more solemn. 'Apparently that's when it can be most dangerous. And, of course, she's never been strong,' he added defensively.

It was Maggie's private opinion that Mrs Hervey could go ten rounds with an ox and win on a knock-out, but she bit back the angry words.

'All she could think of was you,' Robin went on. 'She kept saying to me while we were waiting for the ambulance, ''Poor Margaret will be so disappointed.'' She was nearly in tears.'

'I can imagine,' Maggie said grimly. 'When did all this start?'

'In the early hours of this morning, although she did confess to the doctor that she hadn't been feeling very well for several days. But she said nothing, tried to pretend nothing was wrong, because she didn't want to be a nuisance.'

Maggie's lips parted, then closed again. She knew an overwhelming impulse to seize Robin by his neatly knotted conservative tie and say, 'Your mother has turned being a nuisance into an artform. She is greedy and selfish, and terrified of losing you. She's taken a stock situation from fiction—a cliché that I'd pencil out, screaming, if I came across it in a script—because she knows that I'll recognise it as such and you won't. It's her way of telling me that I can't win. That she's prepared to use the ultimate weapon against me—delicate health.'

'You've gone really pale.' Robin reached out and patted her hand, rather clumsily. 'I knew how concerned you'd be. I tried to think of some way of breaking it to you...'

'Passing on this kind of news is never easy.' Maggie kept her voice neutral with an effort. 'How long does your mother expect to stay in hospital?'

'It's difficult to say, and of course, I have to be on hand in case she needs anything.'

Maggie steeled herself. 'And the doctor's quite sure it is her heart? After all, your mother doesn't have a great deal to occupy herself with when you're not there, and it's easy to—build up symptoms in one's own mind—imagine things...'

Robin's pleasant face hardened perceptibly. 'Just what are you implying? Do I infer that you think my mother has invented this attack, because she's bored in some way? How could you? If you'd seen her—seen the pain she was in—the brave way she was trying to cope. Maggie, I know you're disappointed about the holiday, and I am too, but this really isn't worthy of you.'

There was a silence, then Maggie said quietly, 'No, perhaps not. I apologise.' She forced a smile. 'So much for Mauritius, then,' *Or anywhere else out of your mother's clutches.*

'Oh, but you can still go,' he said quickly. 'The hotel reservation is waiting, after all. It would be a pity to waste it. Mother said so. She said, "Margaret deserves to get away for a rest, somewhere in the sun where she can relax and meet new people."'

'How kind of her.' Anger was beginning to build inside Maggie, and she fought to control it. 'But I wouldn't dream of going without you.' She paused. 'Perhaps, if your mother's condition turns out to be less serious than you fear, we could get a later flight. As you say, they'll keep our room.'

Perhaps the shared room was the crunch as far as Mrs Hervey was concerned. Maybe if we'd booked separate rooms, or even different hotels, she wouldn't have taken quite such drastic action.

'I wish I could be as optimistic.' He gave her an anxious, rather pleading smile. 'Darling, I'm so sorry about all this. But there'll be another time.'

Oh, no, there won't, thought Maggie. Your mother will see to that. This was in the nature of a trial run—to see how you'd react. Now she knows she can pull the strings whenever she wants and you'll dance.

'Of course there will,' she smiled at him, calmly. 'Now I'm sure you want to get back to the hospital—check there haven't been any developments. It was good of you to come over and explain in person.'

He looked aghast. 'But that was the least I could do. Mother insisted.' He hesitated. 'I've checked with my insurance, and we won't be out of pocket over any cancellation. Family illness, you know.' There was another awkward silence, then he looked at his watch. 'Maybe I should be getting back, at that.' He gave her an unhappy look. 'You do understand, don't you? You know how much I was looking forward to being with you.'

'Yes.' As he got to his feet, Maggie rose too, and kissed him gently on the cheek. 'I understand everything.' She paused. 'Give your mother my regards, and tell her I'm sure she'll be feeling much better soon.'

'Thank you.' He rested his hand on her shoulder for a moment. 'You're a wonderful girl, Maggie. A wonderful friend.'

She watched the door close behind him, then slowly and carefully she counted to twenty before picking up her empty cup and throwing it with all her strength at the fireplace. It smashed instantly, sending shards of pottery and dribbles of cold coffee everywhere.

She said, 'And that's that,' and began to cry, hot heavy tears of rage and disappointment. She sank down on her knees on the rug, arms wrapped across her body, and sobbed out loud.

She wasn't crying for the loss of her sunlit, tropical holiday. She was grieving for Robin, and the life with him she had hoped for—planned for. Because she knew with paralysing certainty that even if he were to walk back through that door and propose marriage here and now, she would not accept.

She supposed she should be glad that Mrs Hervey had shown her hand so early in the game. Perhaps one day, she would even be grateful that she had been given the chance to walk away from a potentially monstrous and destructive situation, but not now. Now, she felt stricken, as if her life lay in as many pieces as her ill-used cup.

She wept until she had no tears left, and the harsh, hiccupping sobs gradually died away into silence. She went on kneeling, staring into space, wondering numbly what to do next.

Going to Mauritius by herself was out of the question. The hotel, a luxurious bungalow complex, would be full of couples, which would only serve to emphasise her own sense of loneliness and isolation. Nor could she find anyone else to accompany her at this short notice.

And if I could, I wouldn't want to, she thought. It'll be bad enough when everyone finds out. They'll all be so sympathetic, and falling over themselves not to say, 'I told you so,' especially Louie and Sebastian. I don't think I can bear it.

She supposed she could try to book herself another kind of holiday, somewhere her presence as a single woman wouldn't be quite so remarkable, but her heart wasn't in it. She couldn't think of one place she was remotely interested in going to.

On the other hand, she couldn't stay in London either. Unless she stayed in her flat like a total hermit, news would soon spread that she hadn't gone away, and if she wasn't careful she would be back at the office, wet-nursing Kylie St John through the re-write of her next bestseller.

Oh, no, Maggie thought with sudden violence. Over my dead body.

She got to her feet, drawing a deep breath. There was somewhere else she could go. There was her cottage.

Sebastian might joke about it, but small as it was, and hidden in the wilds of East Anglia, it was precious to her. She enjoyed its seclusion and its comparative inaccessibility down little more than a farm track. She had bought it more or less for a song, using a legacy from her grandmother for the purpose, and over the past few years had poured in most of her spare cash on improvements to the building. She had had a second-hand Aga installed, and had toured the used furniture shops, choosing exactly the right items, then cleaning and stripping them down with loving care. Her next major project was going to be a bathroom. The present toilet arrangements consisted of an outside loo ringed by nettles, a rickety washbasin in the larger of the two bedrooms, and a tin bath in front of the Aga.

Her sister Louie, who had fallen foul of the nettles on a midnight trip to the loo, had said with feeling that the whole place was like the end of the world, and the name had stuck. In fact their last Christmas present to her had been a handsome carved wooden nameplate with the legend 'World's End', which Seb declared had doubled the value of the cottage in one fell swoop.

But as a bolthole—a place to lick her wounds in peace—it was second to none. She could go there—be alone—and get her head together. Start planning for life after Robin.

She winced as she made her way into the bedroom. The first thing she had to do was unpack her case. She wouldn't be needing any glamorous coordinated beachwear at World's End. Jeans, sweaters and thermal undies were the order of the day there.

The worst moment was when she came across the nightgown she had bought for her first night with Robin. It was white, pretty and sheer, and if she was honest, she hadn't counted on wearing it for very long. She had always enjoyed being in Robin's arms, and wanted his kisses. She had grown accustomed to him, felt safe with him, and had no qualms about giving herself to him completely. Now, she looked down at the nightgown, feeling fresh tears scalding in her throat. She never wanted to see it again, or any of the other charming, provocative trifles she had bought either.

Stony-faced, she emptied them all out on to the floor and kicked them to one side. Serves me right for trying to be sexy, she thought, biting her lip. I should have remembered that I'm good old Maggie, and bought some sensible knickers.

She took a long, clinical look at herself in the mirror. She would never set the world on fire, but when her face wasn't streaked with tears, her nose red and swollen, and her grey-green eyes like twin bruises, she was passable, she thought judiciously, even though her hair was common-or-garden red rather than more sophisticated auburn, and she was definitely on the skinny side of slender.

And now unexpectedly back on the market, as estate agents said in their advertisements.

'A wonderful friend,' Robin had said.

Was that really all she had been to him? And would she have been any more in that romantic bungalow, tucked away in a flower-filled tropical garden?

Now we shall never know, she thought with bitter self-derision, rooting through her wardrobe for gear more appropriate to mid-October in England.

She repacked her case, then stripped off her dress and jacket, changing into black wool trousers and a matching polo-necked sweater.

She was half-way out of the door when she remembered the cottage keys. She pulled open the top drawer of the bureau and reached into the corner, but the familiar bunch wasn't there.

Frowning, Maggie pulled the drawer out further, riffling through the contents. But there was no sign of the keys. Had she forgotten to put them away after her last visit, a couple of months ago? It seemed so. No doubt they would be tucked away in some handbag.

But she wouldn't look for them now. She kept a spare set in the bottom tray of the box which stored her costume jewellery. She would take those instead.

She carried her case round to the lock-up garage where she kept her Metro, then dashed round the local mini-market, filling a box with bread, eggs and milk as well as canned goods. She could get meat and vegetables at the farm shop on her way to World's End.

The weather was deteriorating, she noticed, as she began her journey. She switched on the car radio and listened to the forecast. The outlook was stormy, with rain and high winds approaching gale force at times.

Maggie pulled a face. Electricity supplies to the cottage were inclined to be erratic in bad weather, although the gales might never materialise. But if they did, she had plenty of candles, and a fresh supply of fuel for the Aga had been delivered at the beginning of the month, according to Mrs Grice, the farmer's wife, who kept a friendly eye on the cottage for her.

I'll make out, she thought with a mental shrug. And stormy weather suits my mood at the moment. The wind and I can howl together.

Getting out of London was the usual nightmare, and Maggie was a mass of tension by the time she won clear of the suburbs. She had intended to drive straight to the cottage, but now she decided she would take her time—stop for a meal even. It was ages since she had been out to dinner, she realised with amazement. Robin didn't care for restaurant food, so she had usually ended up cooking for him at the flat—except when they had eaten at his mother's house.

She found an Italian restaurant, already filling up with customers, and demolished an enormous plateful of lasagne, washed down with a glass of the house wine, following this with a helping of chocolate fudge cake laden with cream.

Robin, who believed in healthy eating, would have disapproved of every mouthful, and the knowledge gave her a kind of guilty pleasure as she lingered over her cappuccino. Comfort-eating, she thought. When her three weeks in hiding ended, she'd probably be like a barrel.

The wind had risen considerably by the time she started off again. Strong gusts buffeted the car, slowing her journey considerably, and she was half tempted to stop and spend the night at a hotel and hope for better conditions next day.

Oh, to hell with it, she thought. I've come half-way. I may as well go on.

The further she drove, the more she regretted her decision. The rain was battering against the roof and windscreen as if trying to gain access and the wind sounded like some constant moan of torment.

It was nearly midnight before she turned with a sigh of relief on to the track which led to the cottage. Clouds were scudding across the sky like thieves in the night, and the trees which lined the track were swaying violently and groaning as if in pain.

I've never seen it as bad as this, Maggie thought, avoiding a fallen branch. Thank goodness I had the roof mended in the spring.

She parked in her usual spot, grabbed her case, and ran for the front door. The wind tore at her, lifting her almost off her feet, and for a moment she felt helpless in its power and badly frightened. The gust slackened, and she threw herself forward, grasping the heavy metal door-handle to brace herself while she searched in the dark for the keyhole.

At last the door yielded, and she almost fell into the living-room. It was a struggle then to re-close the door. The wind fought her every inch as if it were a living enemy, and her arms were aching by the time she had finished.

Gales, indeed, she muttered to herself. This feels more like a hurricane.

She tried the light switch beside the door without much hope, but to her surprise the central light came on, although it was flickering badly.

Just give me time to find the candles, Maggie appealed silently, going to the small walk-in pantry. As she lifted its latch, it occurred to her how unusually warm the room felt.

It was as if—as if... She stood motionless for a moment, then crossed the room to check. There was no 'if' about it. Someone had lit the Aga.

Mrs Grice sometimes lit it for her, if she knew she was coming down, but this time Maggie hadn't signalled her intentions. So unless Mrs Grice had suddenly been gifted with second sight...

Oh, don't be stupid, Maggie apostrophised herself. She probably thought the place smelled damp and needed airing through. I'll thank her tomorrow.

She found the candles, their pottery holders, and a box of matches, as well as the old-fashioned stone hot water bottle she had picked up in a junk shop. She needed its comfort tonight, she thought, as she filled the kettle and put it to boil on top of the hotplate. She would have some Bovril as well, she decided, taking the jar out of the cupboard.

There was a solitary beaker upside down on the draining-board. Maggie stared at it for a moment, frowning. Where had that come from? she wondered with a frisson of uneasiness.

Now stop it, she caught at herself impatiently, Mrs Grice came and lit your stove for you. Surely you don't grudge her a cup of coffee for her efforts? All the same, it was unusual. Mrs Grice was a meticulous housekeeper, not given to abandoning stray cups on draining-boards.

When the kettle boiled, she filled her bottle, picked up one of the candles and the matches, and mounted the flight of open-tread stairs which led from the living-room to the upper floor. Her bed, she thought, could be warming while she had her Bovril.

She opened her bedroom door, and went in, putting the candlestick down on the dressing-table before turning on the light.

And froze.

Her bed was already occupied. A naked man was lying across it, her brain registered in panic, face downwards, and fast asleep, one arm dangling limply towards the floor.

Maggie could feel the scream starting in the pit of her stomach. By the time it reached her throat, it was a hoarse, wild yell of terror that made itself heard even above the keening of the wind.

The man stirred and half sat up, propping himself on an elbow as he looked dazedly round at her.

She recognised him at once, of course. It had hardly been possible to pick up a newspaper or a magazine for the past eighteen months without seeing his picture. And just lately he'd made the headlines again—for rape.

It was Jay Delaney.

The stone bottle slipped from her nerveless grasp and fell to the floor with a crash that shook the cottage.

And, as if on cue, all the lights finally went out.

CHAPTER TWO

THE darkness closed round her, suffocating her, and Maggie screamed again, hysterically.

She had to find the door, she had to get away, but she felt totally disorientated. She swung round, colliding with the corner of the dressing-table, crying out in pain as well as fear.

'Do us both a favour, lady. Keep still and keep quiet.' Even when angry it was an attractive voice, low, resonant and with a trace of huskiness. Part of his stock in trade, Maggie thought with furious contempt as she rubbed her hip.

She heard the bed creak. Heard him stumble and swear with a vigour and variety she had never experienced before. Then came the rasp of a match and the candle blossomed into flame.

The cottage shook in the grip of another gust, and in the distance Maggie heard a noise like a faint roar. The curtains billowed in the draught, and the shadows danced wildly in the candle's flicker, diminishing the room, making it close in on her. And him.

They looked at each other in inimical silence.

At last, he said, 'Who the hell are you, and how the hell did you find me?'

'Find you?' Maggie flung back her head, returning his glare with interest. 'What makes you think I was even looking?'

'Oh, come off it, sweetheart. What are you—a journalist, or a fan? If you're a reporter—no comment. If you're a groupie, you're out of luck. I'm in no mood for female company, as your own common sense should have told you. Either way, get out, before I throw you out.'

'Save the rough stuff for your tacky series, Mr Delaney,' Maggie said, with gritted teeth. 'You lay one hand on me, and you'll be in jail so fast your feet won't touch the ground. And you won't get bail. That's if I don't have you arrested anyway for breaking and entering.'

His voice was dangerously calm. 'And what precisely am I supposed to have—broken and entered?'

The candle-flame steadied and brightened, the extra illumination providing her with an all too potent and quite unnecessary reminder that he didn't have a stitch on. A fact of which he himself seemed magnificently unconscious as he confronted her, hands on hips.

'My home,' she snarled. 'This house.'

There was a long and tingling silence. Jay Delaney said slowly, 'You must be the sister-in-law.'

'Sister-in-law?' Maggie's voice cracked. 'You mean—Sebastian—told you that you could come here?' Suddenly she remembered the keys so mysteriously missing. Seb knew where they were kept. He must have helped himself on his way out—while she was in the bedroom. 'But he had no right—no right at all...'

'He said there was no problem—that I could hide up here—get a few days' peace. He said this was the end of the world, and that no one would ever

find me here.' He sounded weary. 'You were supposed to be going abroad—Martinique, or some
damned place,' he added almost accusingly.

'Mauritius,' she said tersely. 'But, as you can see,
I'm standing right here.'

Jay Delaney lifted a bare, muscular shoulder in
a laconic shrug. 'Snap.'

'Is that all you have to say?'

'It seems to cover the situation.' His mouth
slanted in a sudden, wry grin.

Maggie drew a sharp, angry breath. 'Then
perhaps you'd care to do the same,' she said with
icy significance, turning her back on him with elab-
orate ostentation.

To her fury, she heard him give a low amused
chuckle. 'Isn't it a little late for outraged modesty?
How old are you, anyway, sister-in-law—twenty-
seven—twenty-eight? I can't be showing anything
you haven't seen before.'

'I'm twenty-four,' she said, stung by his ref-
erence to her age, but at the same time relieved that
he hadn't gauged her total inexperience. 'Not that
it's any concern of yours,' she added belatedly,
listening to the rustle of material and the sound of
a zip closing.

'It's safe to look,' he said softly. 'That's if you
didn't see enough the first time around.'

Sudden colour burned her face as she turned unwillingly back to face him. 'Actually, Mr Delaney,
I would prefer not to see you at all. I want you out
of my house, now.'

'That could be difficult,' he said thoughtfully.
The jeans he had put on were like a second skin,

Maggie thought in outrage. How could he seem marginally less decent clothed than naked?

'Why?' she asked glacially.

'For one thing I have no transport. Sebastian smuggled me out of my hotel and brought me here in a hired car, to fool the Press gang. He's coming back to collect me in time for the next police interview.'

'Then you'll just have to hire a car of your own, and find another refuge.'

'You have no phone here.'

'There's a phone at the farm.'

'But I can hardly turn up on the doorstep demanding to use it at this time of night.' His reasonable tone grated on her. 'Quite apart from the inconvenience I'd be causing, I don't want to draw attention to myself right now.'

'Why change the habits of a lifetime?' Maggie said bitingly.

The firm mouth tightened. 'I thought I'd made it clear that I'm hiding out here. I can't set foot out of doors in London without some tabloid baying for my blood. As long as I can keep my presence here a secret, I'm safe for the time being.'

'And you expect me to sympathise?' Maggie shook her head. 'I said Seb had no right to bring you here, and I meant it. I loathe you, Jay Delaney, and every arrogant, sexist, chauvinist element you stand for. You're totally contemptible. Men like you have got to learn you can't force yourself on unwilling women and get away with it. I hope they lock you, and all rapists, away forever.'

There was another taut silence. 'Brave words,' he said slowly. 'Considering that, at this moment in time, I'm locked away with you. And who appointed you judge and jury, anyway, my little red-haired spitfire?'

'I'm not afraid of you,' she said defiantly.

'No?' Jay Delaney took a step towards her. Then another. His eyes held hers, and his mouth curved in a smile without amusement.

Instinctively, Maggie backed away, and found herself trapped almost immediately against the wall behind her.

'Don't come near me.' Her voice sounded shrill and ragged.

'Why not? According to you, I've already raped one woman, so I might as well be hanged for a sheep as a lamb.' He put a hand on the wall at either side of her body, effectively cutting off any hope of escape.

His eyes—they were incredibly blue, she noticed almost inconsequentially—began a leisurely and insolent inspection of her body, lingering in frank assessment on the small high breasts outlined beneath the cling of the black sweater, then sweeping down to the gentle swell of her hips and the length of her slender thighs.

His scrutiny seemed to sear through her clothes. She suddenly found it difficult to breathe. Her voice cracked. 'Please—let me go.'

'In my own good time,' said Jay Delaney. Using the tip of one forefinger, he lightly, almost casually began to circle the peak of her left breast through her sweater. He did it with aching slowness, letting her nipple harden to taut, greedy life as he touched her. His eyes were dispassionate as they looked into hers.

Maggie leaned back against the wall, palms flattened, fingers splayed against the plaster, as if she was trying to impress herself on it or sink into it completely and be absorbed. Her body felt strangely heavy and her legs were shaking under her.

No one had ever touched her in this way before, and her body clenched in shamed and painful excitement.

What was happening to her, she asked herself dazedly? What was she allowing to happen? This couldn't be real. It had to be some fantasy—some nightmare. She ought to protest—to struggle—to hit out. She couldn't just—stand here, and let him subject her to this intimate torment.

Jay Delaney bent towards her, his lips only inches from hers, the sharp smell of alcohol on his breath. The warmth from his body seemed to envelop her, mingled with the faint scent of some cologne he used.

His hand slid under the ribbed welt of the sweater and caressed the warm, smooth skin above the waistband of her trousers, then stroked upwards to the cleft between her breasts and the tiny plastic clip which fastened her bra at the front. He twisted the clasp, snapping it open, letting the imprisoning lacy cups fall away from her breasts.

Her mouth was dry. Every nerve, every pulse in her body seemed to be suspended in anticipation, waiting to feel the stroke of his fingers on her bare and eager breasts.

But it did not happen.

Instead, Jay Delaney stepped back, pulling her sweater back into place almost with indifference. The blue eyes bored into hers.

He said softly, 'You mentioned something about unwilling women. Do you include yourself in that category?'

She stared at him, trying to speak, trying to think of something to say, but no words would come. Instead, she knew an urge to burst into humiliated tears. She had never behaved like that before— never. Standing there, letting a complete stranger— insult her body.

'Two more things,' he said. 'I hope you, as the owner of this property, are insured, because I may have broken a toe just now, falling over your damned hot water bottle. If I don't walk, I don't work, and my television company may well sue you.'

He picked up a half-empty bottle of Scotch from the night table and poured a measure into the glass beside it.

'And, lastly, observe this. I've been drinking steadily since I got here, so even if half a dozen hired cars turned up at this moment I wouldn't be driving any of them, lady, because I have far too much alcohol in my bloodstream.' He raised the glass to her in a parody of a toast. 'You can do as you please, sweetheart, but I'm going nowhere tonight.'

Her throat muscles worked at last. She said thickly, 'Then I shall leave.'

Jay Delaney shrugged, then stretched out on the bed again, glass in hand. 'That's your privilege.' He sounded almost bored.

Watching him like a hawk, she edged along the wall to the door, found the handle, turned it, and backed on to the landing. He seemed to have lost interest in her, but she didn't trust him—not after the disgusting—the unforgivable way he had treated her.

Down in the living-room, she snatched up her bag from the kitchen table and ran to the door. As she opened it, the wind shrieked into the room, and for a moment she quailed.

Then, biting her lip, she forced herself out into the wildness of the night. Better to face a demon wind, she thought, than stay with that human fiend, currently drinking himself into extinction on her bed.

Battered and buffeted, Maggie had to fight every step of the way to the car. And even when she was in the driver's seat, with the door shut, she didn't feel safe. The car was rocking uneasily with every gust.

She took a deep breath as she started the engine, trying to calculate how far it was to the village. There was a pub there which handled overnight accommodation. They might not be too pleased to have to provide it at one o'clock in the morning, but surely they would understand this was an emergency.

She looked back at the cottage, and the light flickering in the upstairs room. Her sanctuary—and she was being driven away from it.

But only for one night, she thought. Tomorrow she would phone Seb's London office and give her brother-in-law a piece of her mind, making it clear he could come and take Jay Delaney away. And he can think himself lucky I'm not charging him with indecent assault, she thought, fighting back an angry sob.

But the thought of describing what he had done to her to a police officer made her cringe. And there was the question of her own response too. Why hadn't she at least slapped his face?

Damn him, she thought seething. Oh, damn him to hell.

If she had been concentrating more, she would probably have seen the giant elm lying across the track in time. As it was, when it loomed up in the headlights, she hit her brakes a fraction too late, and the Metro ploughed into it with a sickening crunch of metal and broken glass. Maggie was thrown forward, but her seat-belt held her firmly enough. Her ribs were bruised against the steering-wheel, and there was a sharp pain above her right eye, but apart from that she seemed to have got off lightly.

She sat, staring through the shattered wind-screen, unable to believe what had happened.

She thought stupidly, 'There's a tree down. I'll have to move it if I want to get out.'

She released her belt and tried to open her door, but it was jammed because of the impact, and she started to beat on the panels, shaking, and crying out in fear.

'Turn your engine off.' Suddenly Jay Delaney had materialised beside the car, and was shouting at her through the window. She forced her trembling fingers to comply. He gestured at her to wind the window down, and she obeyed.

'It's turning out to be quite a night,' he said grimly, surveying the damage. 'Your insurance company's going to be working overtime. So what's the problem? Door stuck?'

She nodded, her throat working convulsively.

'Then we'll try the passenger door.' He sounded almost soothing. 'And if that doesn't work, we'll get you out through the window, or the hatchback.'

The passenger door opened with a wrench.

'OK,' Jay said. 'Just slide over, and get out.'

'I—don't think I can.'

He said something very rude and derisive under his breath, then leaned into the car, taking her hands in his.

'You can't sit there all night. If one tree's down, others may follow,' he added grimly. 'So move.'

In the end, he had to half drag her from the car.

'Can you walk?'

'I don't know.'

'Then try putting one foot in front of the other, and see what happens.'

That was one of the funniest things she had ever heard, and she began to giggle weakly.

'None of that.' Jay's fingers stung on her cheek, making her gasp. 'Hysterics in the house, not out here.'

There were candles burning on the table and the dresser when they finally stumbled back into the living-room. Jay pulled out a chair and pushed Maggie into it.

He picked up the beaker from the table. 'What's this?'

'I made myself some Bovril.' A thousand years ago.

He grimaced. 'Well, it's cold now.' He tipped it down the sink. 'I prescribe hot milk with a slug of whisky in it.' He paused. 'Not that we have a great deal of milk. Seb only provided me with rations for one.'

'I've brought some groceries.'

'Where are they?'

'In the boot of the car.'

There was a pungent silence, then he said, too politely, 'How unfortunate you didn't mention it a little earlier.'

'They can wait there till tomorrow.'

'They can indeed.' He went upstairs and came back with the whisky. He had put on a sweater, she realised, before he had come to look for her, but in a strange way he still didn't look any more *dressed*. Or did she just think that because she had been forced to see him so blatantly undressed?

She watched him open the cardboard container and pour milk into a saucepan, then put it on to heat.

'You didn't spill any,' she said.

'I'm housetrained. I used to live with a woman who was fussy about things like that.'

'One of your many conquests, no doubt.' And of course he would have to brag about it.

'No,' he said. 'My mother.'

She was taken aback. That sounded altogether too cosy and domestic for someone like Jay Delaney. He was a jungle creature, a predator.

She watched him fill two beakers, add a measure of whisky to each, and bring them to the table.

'Here.' He passed her one.

'I don't like whisky.'

'Tough. Drink it, or I'll pour it down your throat.'

She sipped, shuddering elaborately. Jay seated himself opposite, and watched her sardonically.

'Nice performance,' he commented. 'Are you in our profession?'

'No, I'm in publishing.'

'Let me guess.' He pretended to think, then snapped his fingers. 'Virago Books.'

She gave him a stony look. 'Munroe and Craig, actually. We're a fairly new imprint.'

'Presumably, you're neither Munroe nor Craig.'

'No. I'm Maggie—Margaret Carlyle. I'm an editor.'

'And an editor who should be in Mauritius.'

She bit her lip, and drank some more milk. In spite of her dislike of the taste she had to admit that there was a new warmth stealing through her veins, dispelling the trembling and the cold.

'So,' he went on. 'What are you doing here, Maggie Carlyle?'

'This is my house,' she said curtly. 'I don't owe you any explanations.'

There was a silence. Then he said, 'Let us agree that under normal circumstances, neither of us would wish to spend even five minutes in each other's company. Yes?'

Maggie nodded, staring down at her beaker.

'But circumstances are not normal, and whether we like it or not, we are stuck here together under the same roof, maybe for an indefinite period, so we may as well be civil to each other. Right?'

'Not necessarily,' she objected. 'This storm won't last forever. You can leave tomorrow.'

'On foot?' He gave her a steady look. 'Lady, you aren't even trying to be reasonable.'

She put down the beaker. 'Is that how you'd describe some of your conduct tonight?' Her voice sounded aggravatingly breathless suddenly. 'Reasonable?'

'I was just teaching you a much-needed lesson, sweetheart,' he said levelly. 'Don't give it out, if you're not prepared to take it. Maybe you'll think twice next time before slagging me off about my supposed sins.'

'There isn't a great deal of supposition involved,' she said coldly. 'They've been fairly well documented.'

Jay leaned back, tilting his chair, surveying her through narrowed eyes. 'You really like to live dangerously, don't you, darling? Be warned, the next lesson will be administered to your backside, with the flat of my hand.'

'Very macho,' Maggie said with contempt. 'Are you really pretending, Mr Delaney, that you don't like your hard-won reputation as a hell-raiser?'

'You deal with works of fiction every day of your life,' Jay said with a shrug. 'So how is it you believe everything you read in the newspapers?'

'There's no smoke without fire.' She really couldn't believe she had said that, and by the look of unholy amusement on his face neither could he.

'That's a novel thought,' he said. 'Did one of your authors write it?'

'No,' she said shortly. 'It probably came from one of your television series.' She pushed her chair back, and stood up. 'And now I'm going up to bed, in my own spare room.' She paused. 'The door locks, and I don't wish to be disturbed on any pretext.'

'Don't flatter yourself,' Jay drawled. 'If you'd really been following the reports of my private life, you'd know my taste doesn't run to under-developed redheads.' He got to his feet. 'Before you go, do you have a first-aid kit around?'

'Of course,' Maggie said curtly, still smarting from 'under-developed'. 'Why, do you want to splint your broken toe?'

'No, I'm thinking of taping over your mouth,' he said with a certain grimness. 'As it happens, you've cut your forehead. It needs cleaning up.'

'Cut?' Maggie remembered the sharp pain after the collision and put up a hand, encountering a faint stickiness. 'Is it bad?'

'Plastic surgeons can do miracles these days,' he said gravely. 'But for now, let's see how we go with some antiseptic and a sticking-plaster.'

'Oh, stop it.' She glared at him. 'It's all a big joke to you—but this has been one of the worst days and the worst nights of my life.'

'Whereas my own existence is just perfect at the moment, of course.' His mouth twisted. 'But if you want to spend the next few days wallowing in gloom and self-pity, it's all right with me. Shall I attend to that cut first, or would you prefer blood poisoning in your present mood?'

She stood for a long mutinous minute, eyeing him, then trailed into the pantry and came back with the first-aid box. He was filling a basin with hot water from the kettle.

'Thank you,' she said stiltedly.

'Don't go overboard with the gratitude,' he advised. 'I promise this is going to hurt you far more than it hurts me.'

She endured his ministrations with gritted teeth.

'Does it need a stitch?'

'Well, it certainly isn't going to get one.' He applied a small piece of plaster. 'The bandages can come off in a fortnight.' He emptied the basin. 'And, by the way, I'm not going to add to your list of grievances against me by turning you out of your bed. I'll sleep in the spare room.'

She said quickly, 'It's all right. I don't mind. Anyway, it's rather too late to start changing sheets.'

'Yours having been hopelessly contaminated by my fleeting presence, I suppose,' he said, too evenly.

'Not at all,' Maggie protested unconvincingly, a betraying blush spreading up to her hairline.

Jay gave her a bleak look. 'You, lady, are something else,' he said.

He turned away and went up the stairs, and presently she heard the bedroom door bang.

She went round the living-room, tidying things, extinguishing all the candles except the one she would take upstairs with her.

And in spite of Jay's avowal, she would still lock her door, she thought defiantly.

She supposed grudgingly that he had been kind enough, after the accident, but it didn't change a thing. She still despised him and everything he stood for. And although she might be obliged to give him sanctuary tonight, there was no way she was going to share a roof with him again tomorrow.

Another fierce gust shook the house, and she shivered. Always supposing, she thought wryly, that there was any roof left to share.

She paused as a further thought occurred to her, then crossed to the sink unit. Opening the drawer, she extracted the sharpest long-bladed kitchen knife she possessed. He had already shown he couldn't be trusted, she told herself. And she was entitled to protect herself.

She went slowly and gingerly up the stairs, protecting the candle-flame. Her room—his room—was in darkness, and she paused for a moment at the door, listening, wondering if he was safely asleep, anaesthetised by whisky.

His voice reached her, quietly and mockingly, 'Goodnight, Maggie Carlyle. Pleasant dreams.'

She started so violently she nearly dropped the knife, and the candle-flame wavered and went out.

Cursing under her breath, she felt her way along the landing to the spare room. She found a match and relit the candle, putting it on the small chest of drawers, before turning the key in the lock.

The narrow single bed looked singularly uninviting. And there was a small solid hump in the middle of it.

Maggie pulled back the duvet and found herself staring down at the stone hot water bottle. For a moment she stood, motionless, then she sat down on the edge of the bed, buried her face in her hands, and began to cry.

It was an uncomfortable night. The noise of the storm was unabating, and several times Maggie was terrified that the window was going to blow in.

In spite of the reassurance of the knife under her pillow, she was still uneasily on tenterhooks, wondering what she would do if he forced an entry to her room and she was actually obliged to use it.

She was still debating the issue when she fell into an exhausted sleep just before dawn.

It was daylight when she finally opened bleary eyes on the world. The sky outside the window looked grey and angry, she realised shuddering, and the wind was still blowing fiercely.

She crawled out of bed and dragged on the trousers and sweater she had been wearing the previous night. Along with her bed, she had also sacrificed the washbasin, she realised crossly. She would have to perform her morning ablutions downstairs in the sink.

She had a lot to do today, she thought sombrely. She would have to notify Mr Grice about the fallen tree, and get him to phone the local garage to take her car away. She would also need to contact her insurance company.

And taking absolute priority over all these was the necessity to get Jay Delaney out of the cottage, and out of her life.

He wasn't in the living-room when she went downstairs, and she seized the opportunity of the unexpected privacy to wash her face and hands and clean her teeth. When he had gone, she decided, she would lock the door, draw the curtains and get out the tin bath.

She was ashamed of the crying jag she had embarked on last night, she thought, as she filled the kettle and set it to boil, but in a way it was understandable. She had built such hopes and such dreams on that trip to Mauritius—and on her first night alone with Robin—that the situation at World's End seemed a brutal anti-climax.

And if she was honest, finding the hot water bottle like that had been the final straw. An unlooked-for kindness from an unexpected source. An unwanted kindness, too, she reminded herself. If Jay Delaney thought he could creep into her good graces by such means, then he could think again.

He said from the doorway, 'Have you got any weed-killer?' making her jump all over again.

'What for?' she demanded suspiciously, when her heartbeat had settled down.

'How about a suicide pact?' he said pleasantly. 'Actually, I thought I'd have a go at the nettles round the john. Going for a pee in this establishment is like embarking on a survival course with the SAS.'

Maggie's lips were parting to say, 'Well, no one else has ever complained,' when he added, 'Thank goodness Sebastian warned me what to expect,' and she had to switch smartly to Plan B.

'I'm sorry I can't provide the gold-plated five-star amenities you're accustomed to,' she said sweetly.

'The service is lousy too,' he said. 'I'm used to coffee in bed.'

'You'll have to wait till I find the weedkiller.'

'I wish I could think you were joking.' He paused. 'You've lost quite a few tiles off the roof. If it starts to rain, you could be in trouble.'

'I think I have enough problems already.' She went outside to check, and whistled in dismay. 'Damnation. I spent a fortune on that roof only a few months ago.'

'What rank ingratitude these inanimate objects often display,' he said sympathetically.

'Very amusing—when it's not your roof.' She picked up an unbroken tile and eyed it and then him with a certain amount of speculation. 'It's possible, you know, to make running repairs, by—pushing tiles back into place.'

'Wouldn't you need incredibly long arms?'

Maggie gave him a brief, flat smile. 'Try a medium-sized ladder instead. There's one in the lean-to.'

Jay's brows lifted. 'Am I hearing this properly? Are you suggesting I should go up on your roof and stick back these loose tiles?'

'Right first time.'

'No way.'

'Why not?'

'I'm scared of heights.'

'Rubbish,' she said roundly. 'I'm told Hal McGuire is always leaping round other people's roofs, a hundred feet up in the air.'

'Hal McGuire's stunt man, certainly. I can't even bear to watch all that stuff. I stay in the caravan, and learn my lines.'

'You're a wimp.'

'I'm an actor. A very expensive, very successful, classically trained actor. Ask me to fight a duel for you, and I'll astound you.'

'I doubt it,' Maggie said shortly. 'Honestly, it isn't even a very high roof.'

'I get vertigo on chairs. Besides, a broken toe is one thing. A broken neck can be serious.'

'Could you bring yourself to hold the ladder for me, then?'

'If I'm allowed to keep my eyes shut.'

'Oh, for Pete's sake,' Maggie exploded in disgust and stalked off to fetch the ladder.

Jay followed and took it from her. 'I'll make a deal with you. I'll risk terminal terror in exchange for scrambled eggs and coffee. But they'd better be good.'

Maggie bit her lip. The last thing she had planned on doing was cooking for her unwanted guest. Getting him up on the roof had seemed simply a way of keeping him occupied while she walked over the fields to the farm and made arrangements for his departure.

But if he seriously intended to replace some of the fallen tiles, she supposed reluctantly that she owed him some breakfast in return.

She nodded abruptly. 'All right. It's a deal.' She paused. 'I'd better go to the car and get those supplies.'

She shrugged on a quilted jacket, collected her keys and set off down the track. It wasn't easy. Every step of the way was littered with fallen branches and other debris. She moved as much as she could back towards the hedge, but some of the larger branches defeated her. She was hot and out of breath by the time she reached the car and got the boot open.

She was lifting out the first box when she heard a man's voice call to her.

Looking up, she saw Mr Grice coming down the track on the far side of the tree.

'Good morning,' she called back. 'Terrible storm, wasn't it?'

'Worse than that, seemingly,' the farmer said as he reached her. 'They're calling it a hurricane. There's been people killed—houses blown down, and fallen trees everywhere. My lads have gone out with the tractor to lend a hand on the main road. The missus said she thought she'd seen a car, although she wasn't sure it were yourn, come down here yesterday, so I reckoned I'd come and check— see you were all right.'

'Yes, I'm fine, apart from the Metro.' It must have been Sebastian's hired car Mrs Grice had spotted. 'Mr Grice, could I come up later—use the phone?'

He chuckled. 'You'll be lucky, m'dear. Phone's dead as a doornail, and all the power's off. No one seems to know rightly when it'll be back on either.'

'But I've got to contact a garage,' Maggie said desperately. 'My car needs to be towed away, and I want transport back to London urgently.'

'You forget all about that,' Mr Grice said firmly. 'No one with any sense is going to London today, or anywhere else either. Why, London's been hit worse than anywhere. They reckon not even trains can get in. And all the roads round here are blocked.' He shook his head. 'Terrible, it is. You'd best bide where you are, till things get easier. The missus and I won't let you starve. I'll get young Dave to bring you over some meat and a few veg. How's that?'

Maggie slumped weakly against the rear of the car. 'But I've got to get out of here. You don't understand...'

'It's you that doesn't understand, m'dear. There's an emergency on. People have been hurt—lost their homes, and police are advising everyone not to travel. And it'll be a day or two before we can get round to clearing this track anyway, I reckon, so you'll just have to be patient. I'll send Dave down later with your food.'

He thinks I'm just making a silly feminine fuss about nothing, Maggie thought wretchedly as Mr Grice strode off.

But I'm not, she wanted to scream after him. I'm trapped here with a man—a stranger, who's facing a charge of rape already—and I'm scared stiff. I don't want to be alone with him for another night. I don't.

Yet it seemed the choice was no longer hers. Maggie looked up at the grey, threatening sky, and shivered.

Oh, lord, she thought frantically, what am I going to do?

CHAPTER THREE

SCRAMBLED eggs were not Maggie's *forte*, but these seemed to have turned out better than usual, she thought, as she served them on to the warm plates, and placed them on the table with the cafetiere.

'Ready,' she said shortly to Jay, who was washing his hands at the sink.

'Thank you.' As he sat down, Jay reached across and deftly swapped her plate for his.

'What on earth do you think you're doing?'

'Just a precaution,' he said equably. 'You're a formidable young woman, Ms Carlyle. Don't think I haven't noticed.'

But I didn't think of doctoring his food, Maggie thought grimly, as she tackled her eggs. Why didn't I think of it? And why don't I have a medicine cabinet full of sleeping-pills or strong laxatives to do it with?

As they ate, she found she was studying him covertly under her lashes. So this was the image of heroism in the eighties, she thought contemptuously. He was by no means conventionally handsome. He had a tough, arrogant face, the strong lines of his mouth and jaw accentuated by the obligatory designer stubble. His chestnut hair was overlong, she thought disapprovingly, waving, as it did, below the collar of his checked shirt, which, typically, had one button too many undone, reviving memories she would prefer to banish forever.

His eyes were his best feature, vividly blue and long-lashed, but she still found it impossible to understand why he was regarded as a sex symbol, or why *McGuire* was so often at the top of the TV ratings.

He was pale beneath his tan, and looked faintly haggard altogether this morning, she thought. Suffering a hangover from all the previous night's whisky, no doubt. What a pity his adoring fans couldn't see him now.

He looked up suddenly, and caught her watching him. Embarrassed, Maggie hurried into speech.

'Have you finished on the roof?'

'I certainly hope so. I'd say it was temporarily watertight again, but you'll need to get an expert to look at it.'

'I think all the roofing contractors are going to have more work than they can handle for the foreseeable future. I seem to have got off relatively lightly.' Maggie paused. 'I've been listening to the radio. All the news is terrible. They say Kew Gardens has been devastated—all kinds of rare trees and shrubs destroyed.'

Jay grimaced as he poured himself some coffee. 'A veritable ill wind,' he commented. 'What's the situation locally? Do we know?'

'I spoke to the farmer.' Maggie looked down at her plate. 'Apparently the police are advising people to stay where they are. The roads are blocked, and there aren't any trains either. No one can get in or out.'

'Then we stay here,' he said with a faint shrug.

'As simple as that,' she said bitterly.

'Whinging won't improve matters.'

'I am not whinging.' Maggie hit the table with her fist, making the crockery rattle. 'I came here because I wanted to be alone.'

'So did I. But fate decreed otherwise.'

'Fate be damned,' she said stormily. 'I have Sebastian to thank for all this.'

'You can hardly blame him entirely. After all, he thought you were going to be in Mauritius, and that the cottage would be standing empty.'

'He didn't even have the decency to ask my permission.'

'Probably because he knew it wouldn't be given.' Jay pushed his empty plate away from him, and gave her a straight look. 'Even before we met, I was hardly the flavour of the month with you. Was I?'

'You could hardly expect to be. I dislike men who have no respect for women.'

'And I believe respect has to be earned, no matter what gender you are,' Jay retorted flatly. 'I'm also in favour of giving people the benefit of the doubt. Maybe that's something you should consider.'

'I have no doubts about you,' she said. 'Not any more. Not after the despicable way you treated me last night.'

'I thought I hadn't heard the last of that,' he said reflectively. 'As I told you, I intended to teach you a mild lesson, no more. The fact that it could have easily become very much more was as much a surprise to me as it was to you.'

'How dare you?'

'I dare quite easily. I stopped touching you last night, lady, because I found I was enjoying it far too much, which wasn't the purpose of the exercise at all. Your skin is like warm silk, Maggie Carlyle. Has no one ever told you that? I wanted to run my hands over every inch of you.' He paused. 'And that was just for starters.'

'You are—disgusting,' she said thickly.

Jay shrugged. 'I'm honest. What you discovered last night, Ms Carlyle, is that the brain can't always control the body's more basic reactions.' He smiled reminiscently. 'You were like a kid in a candy store,' he said softly. 'Wanting everything around you.'

'That's not true.' Her voice cracked in outrage.

'Isn't it? So, let's test your candour. If I'd obeyed my baser instincts last night and carried on with what I was doing—if I'd seriously tried to undress you—kissed you—at what point would you have called a halt?'

'At once.'

'Really?' His grin was totally cynical. 'Care to prove your brave words by repeating the experiment?'

'No, I would not,' Maggie said between her teeth. 'I found the whole incident nauseating.'

He poured himself some more coffee, eyeing her meditatively. 'An interesting reaction. Is it sex in general which turns you off, or the prospect of having it with me?'

'There is no prospect of that,' she said. 'In fact, it isn't even a remote possibility.'

'Too true,' he said equably. 'Unless I ask you. And I have no immediate plans to invite you to bed.'

'Am I supposed to find that reassuring?' She drew a quivering breath. 'Your arrogance is appalling. And if you dare lay another hand on me...' She hesitated.

'Yes?' he prompted. 'What will you do?'

She flung back her head. 'I'll make you sorry, that's all.'

'I'm deeply repentant already,' he said. 'But you don't have to worry, Ms Carlyle. Whether you believe it or not, I've never forced myself on a woman yet. I've never found it necessary. And you won't make me break that excellent rule.'

'What a pity that poor girl—Debbie Burrows—can't hear you say that.' Maggie's tone was heavily sarcastic.

'Don't worry—she will—when the case comes to court.' He paused, then added flatly, 'If it does.'

'I suppose you'll try and pressure her to drop her case,' Maggie said with contempt. 'How wonderful it must be to have money and power.'

'Miss Burrows is being backed financially by a Sunday newspaper. She won't be short of cash at the moment. Of course, that may change when they discover she's a pathological liar.'

'I hope she wins,' Maggie said breathlessly. 'I hope they put you in prison for the rest of your life.'

'I really believe you do. As it happens, I feel as if my sentence has started already.' He pushed his chair back, and got to his feet, stretching lithely.

'Well, thanks for the breakfast, Ms Carlyle. I'm glad it's only your tongue that's poisoned,' he added silkily. 'I'm going for a walk across the fields now. When I return, I suggest we should declare some kind of truce. Because whether we like it or not—and it's just as much a hardship for me as for you, believe me—we're stuck with each other for the duration.' He gave her a brief, wintry smile. 'Think about it.'

She could think about nothing else, she thought tautly, as the cottage door closed behind him.

She was being asked to endure the unendurable, she argued with herself. The cottage was too small to permit them to avoid each other, unless she spent the greater part of her time in the seclusion of the spare room. She grimaced, knowing that she would find that unbearable too.

She supposed reluctantly that his proposal of a truce was the only answer, although the thought of the awful kind of artificial intimacy that would impose made Maggie cringe.

For a moment, she sat staring into space, her nails curling like claws into the soft palms of her hands, as she remembered the things he had said to her—what he had implied. *A kid in a candy store.* The memory made her writhe.

It's not true, she insisted to herself. It isn't. I was in a state of shock—that's all. I wasn't myself. I was upset over Robin—missing him.

But Robin never made you feel like that, said a small sly voice in her head. With Robin, you felt secure—contented. Making love with him would have been a normal pleasant progression in the relationship. But the thought of it was never a burning ache—a hunger—coming between you and sleep.

A deep flush of shame swept over her. It wasn't just the storm, or the narrow bed which had disturbed her last night, she was forced to acknowledge. For the first time in her life, sexual curiosity—sexual need—had kept her awake.

And it was all the fault of that—creature. That arrogant, womanising bastard, Jay Delaney.

And he had known exactly what he was doing to her—known, and been able to draw back. That, somehow, was the worst—the most humiliating thing of all.

She got abruptly to her feet, clattering the plates together, angrily aware that her hands were shaking.

A mild lesson. Yet, brief as it had been, it had taught her things about herself that she'd never imagined. Never wanted to know.

And now nothing would ever be the same again.

The sound of the doorlatch made her jump like a scalded cat, and one of the beakers slipped from her hand, cracking against the side of the sink.

'Damnation,' she muttered under her breath. 'That was a short walk,' she said, acidly, as she turned, then stopped abruptly, confronted by the stocky figure of Dave Arnold, who worked at the farm. 'Oh, it's you.'

She forced a smile, wishing that she could like him better. He was about the same age as herself, and not bad-looking in a coarse way. When she'd first moved into the cottage, he had come down at Mr Grice's behest to help her get her furniture settled, and she had been grateful for that, but afterwards he'd persisted in hanging around, making excuses to come to the cottage, and eventually she had had to tell him bluntly to leave her in peace.

He seemed to have accepted that, but she still felt uneasy in his presence, and wished that either Mike or Alan, the Grices' sons, could have made the delivery instead.

'I brought you some food.' He placed two loaded carrier bags on the table. 'Who was you expecting?'

She shrugged evasively, 'Oh, no one in particular. Did Mr Grice put a bill in?'

'I've got it here.' He produced a folded piece of paper from his anorak pocket. 'Got someone staying, have you? I seen a bloke on your roof, earlier.'

'I lost some tiles in the gale,' she said non-committally.

'I'd've put 'em back for you, if you'd asked.'

'Well, now you won't have to. And I'm sure there's a lot to do at the farm.' She sounded brisk and school-mistressy, she realised.

'Funny thing was—I thought I knew him—that bloke on your roof. Thought I'd seen him somewhere before. Been down here other times, has he, then?'

Mind your own bloody business, Maggie told him silently. Aloud, she said, 'I often have people to stay. Will you tell Mr Grice I'll drop off a cheque for all the food when I leave? Now, if you'll excuse me . . .' She began to run water into the sink.

'Funny, though, me thinking I knew him.'

'Hilarious.' Maggie squirted detergent into the water, and whisked it to a foam with her hand, letting her back tell him the interview was over. He accepted his dismissal, and presently she saw him mooching off down the track, on his way back to the farm.

She unpacked the carriers. The Grices had done her proud, she discovered. There was a chicken, some steaks and a small leg of lamb, as well as a home-made meat and potato pie carefully wrapped in greaseproof paper. Hurricane or not, Mrs Grice had been baking.

She put the meat and vegetables away in the pantry, then made another pot of coffee. While she was waiting for it to brew, she sat in the rocking chair beside the Aga, staring into space.

When she heard the door open she didn't even look round. She knew who it was, her whole body tingling in a frightening awareness. Her fingers clenched round the beaker she was holding.

Her voice strove for normality. 'Would you like some coffee?'

'Thank you,' he said with cool politeness. She watched him help himself.

She said, 'One of the men was here from the farm. He saw you on the roof earlier, and he recognised you, although he hasn't placed you yet.'

'You should have jogged his memory,' Jay said after a pause. 'Told him that I was "McGuire" and that several newspapers would pay a lot of money to know where I am. That would have got me out of your hair.'

'Yes,' she said slowly, still not looking at him. 'That's what I should have done.'

'Then why didn't you?'

'I don't know. It—didn't occur to me about the newspapers.'

'An opportunity missed.' He drank some coffee, his eyes never leaving her face. 'To regain your precious solitude.'

'The roads will re-open soon. Then I can go back to London.'

'Where you live alone?'

The curious note in his voice made her flush. 'Is there something unusual about that?'

He shrugged. 'You certainly seem to enjoy your own company, Ms Carlyle. Take this place, which is clearly intended for sole occupation. One easy chair by the stove, one comfortable bed upstairs.' He paused again. 'Were you going to Mauritius on your own too?'

'No, I was not.' Maggie lifted her chin. 'I was going with a friend. A man,' she added, and instantly despised herself for doing so.

'Well, well,' he said softly. 'So the lady has her human side, after all. What went wrong?'

She hesitated. 'His mother was taken ill at the last minute.' She gave him a defensive look. 'Make a joke about that.'

'I wouldn't dream of it. He's clearly a devoted son.' His mouth twisted slightly. 'But maybe not such an ardent lover. Think about it.'

'I've thought about nothing else,' Maggie said, untruthfully.

She hadn't had time to think about Robin. There had been too much else on her mind, too much happening, she realised with faint incredulity. Yet for months now he'd been the most important person in her life.

In fact, he had been the only person in her life. There'd been work, and there'd been Robin. Concerts, theatres, car trips and meals at her flat. Settled, safe and—cosy.

The holiday in Mauritius had been something else. It would have broken the domestic mould, taken them both on a step into the unknown together. It had represented a kind of danger, she thought suddenly, and maybe even without his mother Robin would have backed away at the last moment. Perhaps their relationship wasn't ready for that kind of intimacy. Perhaps it never would have been.

But there was danger everywhere. She hadn't had to go half-way round the globe to find it. It had been waiting for her—here at World's End. She shivered.

'Do I take it then that our truce has been declared?' Jay asked quietly, and she nodded in silent reluctance, getting to her feet.

He held out his hand, but she pretended not to notice, making a business of pouring more coffee for herself. It occurred to her with terrifying force that she dared not risk even the slightest physical contact with him.

'There—doesn't seem a great deal of choice at the moment.'

'Spoken with your usual graciousness.' He was silent for a moment. 'Well, as I'm going to be around for a while, I'll deal with those nettles.' He gave her an edged smile. 'Leaving you free to enjoy your solitude in any way you wish.'

'A broken neck this morning, and nettle rash this afternoon. You are living dangerously, Mr Delaney. I'm sure Hal McGuire would be proud of you.'

'It might be wiser not to speculate on McGuire's reactions to the current situation,' Jay drawled, his eyes sliding insolently down her body. 'The scripts I'm offered don't usually include platonic relationships.'

She glared at him. 'Perhaps they should. Maybe that would have cured you of the delusion that you're irresistible.'

'And what about your own delusion, Ms Carlyle, that you're immune? How do we find a cure for that?'

Maggie bit her lip. 'We don't. And I find this conversation thoroughly distasteful.'

'You began it. And as I suggested last night, it's wiser not to start something you can't finish.' He gave her a level look, before walking to the door.

It seemed very quiet when he had gone. Maggie found she didn't really want the rest of her coffee, and poured it down the sink. She began to wander restively round the room.

The next twenty-four hours, or even—heaven forbid—couple of days promised to be among the most tricky she would ever experience. Like treading on eggshells, she thought, or through a live minefield.

I'd better establish some ground rules, she decided uneasily. And speaking only when spoken to might be a good start.

How was it, she wondered, that an arrogant chauvinist brute like Jay Delaney always seemed able to place her at a disadvantage—put her in the wrong? Although that wasn't the worst of it. Loathsome as the idea was, Maggie couldn't deny that he had the ability to make her physically aware of him as no one had ever done before. The circumstances of their meeting, and their enforced proximity ever since, had made that inevitable, she supposed with reluctance, but certainly no less shameful.

When I get my hands on Sebastian, she planned, seething, brother-in-law or not, I'm going to kill him for doing this to me.

But somehow she had to fill in the hours until Seb's murder. She couldn't spend all her time at World's End, prowling round, brooding over her manifold wrongs.

She prepared some vegetables to go with the meat and potato pie for supper, then settled to some heavy-duty cleaning of the living-room. It didn't really need it, but she badly needed an outlet for her suppressed energies and her temper. Many of her contemporaries dismissed housework as a form of male-inflicted slavery, but Maggie had always obtained a curious satisfaction from making her immediate domain gleam from scrubbing, polishing and window-shining. To her relief the electricity supply was suddenly restored during the afternoon, so she was even able to vacuum.

Housework couldn't make her forget her present situation, but it set it at a safe distance for a while, and she was grateful for that at least.

She had just finished rearranging some dried flowers she had brought to the cottage on her last visit as a centrepiece for the living-room table when Jay returned with the news that it was raining again.

'Oh,' she said, dismayed. 'Do you think it will delay the clearing-up operations?'

'Not for a moment,' he said. 'Except within a hundred-yard radius of this house. My landscape gardening is over for the day.'

He sat down, inspecting a scratch on his hand.

'Were you stung?'

'Inevitably,' he said. 'But not terminally.'

Maggie pushed a tress of hair back from her forehead. She felt hot and sticky after her endeavours, although there was a solution to that, she realised with reluctance. Not, however, an exclusive solution.

She said constrictedly, 'Would—would you like a bath—before we have our evening meal?'

'I think I need one,' Jay said with a grimace. He glanced round. 'But how? The bedroom basin is rather small for total immersion, so is there some secret annexe you haven't yet revealed to me, or do I just strip and stand in the rain with a bar of soap?'

Maggie bit her lip. 'None of those, actually. There's a tub in the shed. I just—fill it with a jug, and bathe in front of the Aga.'

'How very cosy,' Jay drawled.

She took a breath. 'Of course, under the circumstances, there'll have to be a certain amount of—co-operation...'

'Naturally.' He gave her a ferocious leer. 'Shall I scrub your back first or you mine?'

'Neither,' Maggie snapped. 'I was talking about respecting each other's privacy by remaining upstairs for as long as necessary.'

'But I enjoy certain refinements at bath time,' Jay said softly. 'Like—more hot water at intervals, and having a drink brought to me.'

'Then you'll have to fetch them yourself.' To her fury Maggie felt a warm wave of colour sweep into her face, prompted by the image he had evoked. 'This isn't the Ritz. And I'm not your servant.'

'Pity.' Jay grinned at her. 'You don't fancy playing the role of willing and submissive handmaiden for one evening, I suppose? It could add a whole new dimension to your personality.'

'I'll leave my personality the way it is,' she said curtly. 'And it would do wonders for yours if you'd drop the sexual harassment for the next twenty-four hours. With a court case pending, I should have thought you'd have learned your lesson by now.'

'And with a court case pending, I'm amazed you should suggest intimacies like bath time in front of the stove,' he retorted, 'Or are you planning to lock me in the bedroom in case my instincts as a sex maniac take over, and I rush down here and have you by force in a very large puddle?'

In spite of anything she could do, Maggie felt her lips twitch.

'No,' she said, fighting an urge to laugh out loud. 'I don't think that.'

'Thanks for the vote of confidence,' he said drily. 'So—would you like me to fetch the tub and fill it for you?'

'You're the guest,' she said. 'You can have the first turn. I'll get you a towel.' She took the big enamel jug she used for filling the bath from the cupboard under the sink, and put it on the table. 'You see—every modern convenience.'

When she returned downstairs with the towel, the tub was already in position, and Jay, bare to the waist, was occupied in filling it.

'It's larger than I thought,' he remarked, giving her a sideways glance. 'Sure you don't want to economise on hot water by sharing?'

'Quite sure.' Maggie realised with shock that she had been staring at him, absorbing almost avidly the width of his shoulders and the tanned muscularity of his long back. And his remark revealed that he was aware of it too, she thought with chagrin.

She hurried into speech. 'When you've finished, if you could drag the tub to the door, and empty it down the drain just outside, then—call me.'

'No problem.' Jay put down the jug, and began to unbuckle the belt of his jeans. His eyes met hers, held them for a long enigmatic moment.

Maggie's mouth was suddenly dry. She could feel her heart thudding against her ribcage. Felt sure its hammering must be audible in the heavy stillness of the room.

She was aware that all she had to do was stand where she was, and that all further decisions would be made for her. But, dear heaven, just what was she contemplating?

Reality came surging back with the force of a body blow, mingling panic with self-disgust. Maggie turned and headed blindly for the stairs, and the illusion of safety they seemed to offer. Nor did she risk even one fleeting glance over her shoulder, or pause for breath until she was in her bedroom with the door closed behind her.

CHAPTER FOUR

MAGGIE sat on the edge of her bed and stared into space.

She whispered into the unresponsive silence, 'What's the matter with me? What's happening to me?'

But none of the answers which forced themselves to the surface of her confused emotions were any comfort at all.

It was all to do with her disappointment over the trip to Mauritius, she told herself forcefully. It had to be that. She had looked forward to being with Robin—belonging to him at last—and it had made her vulnerable.

She shivered a little, trying to visualise Robin and herself alone together, sharing all the intimacies of lovers. She had assumed their feelings for each other would have smoothed out any difficulties or awkwardness, but now she wasn't so sure it would have been that easy. She attempted to envisage them taking a bath or a shower together, but failed. In fact, she couldn't even imagine Robin suggesting such a thing. He had fairly strict views on hygiene, she recalled unwillingly.

But then her own outlook had been pretty conventional too—before the hurricane. Before her entire world had been turned upside down.

She looked down at her hands, clenched tightly together in her lap. She supposed she should think herself lucky that Jay hadn't followed her—tried to persuade her in some way—pressured her even. She would have only had herself to blame, gazing at him like that—remembering.

A kid in a candy store. That was what he had called her, derisively, and it was totally humiliating to have to admit that the remark held a certain amount of justice.

But was she wholly to blame? One of the things that made Jay Delaney a top-rated TV star was his dynamic appeal to women's sexual fantasies. And off-camera, as she was discovering to her cost, his magnetism was even more potent.

Oh, damn him, she wailed inwardly. And damn the storm which had swept them inexorably together.

The brief tap on her door nearly made her jump out of her skin.

'Yes?' To her annoyance, her voice sounded very young and breathless.

'It's all yours.' His tone through the stout wooden panels was laconic, and he made no attempt to gain admittance. She heard him move away, and the other door close. There was an odd finality in the sound, as if he was trying to tell her, without words, that she had nothing to fear.

She collected her toilet bag and towel, and stepped out on to the landing.

Although there was still no excuse for the Debbie Burrows incident, she could begin to see how it might have happened.

Probably the girl had been carried away by his undoubted glamour and powerful sexual charisma, she thought, biting her lip, and found too late that the point of no return had been reached, and passed. He wasn't innocent, she decided, but perhaps he wasn't totally culpable either.

When she got down to the living-room, she found that Jay had refilled the tub for her. She added a capful of scented essence to the gently steaming water, and swirled it round with her hand.

It was a kind thing for him to have done, she thought, but, like the closing door, it could also be a way of distancing himself—of denying that those few fraught moments between them had ever existed.

Maybe he was remembering Debbie Burrows too—and the fact that in his position he couldn't even contemplate taking a similar risk.

In a way that should have been reassuring, but as she undressed she found she was constantly stopping to listen for sounds of movement overhead.

Oh, for heaven's sake, she adjured herself derisively. What are you expecting him to do? Pace up and down in frustration—like a caged lion or something? Stop being paranoid.

She scooped her hair up on top of her head, secured it with a couple of combs, then slid into the water with a little sigh of pleasure. She let herself relax for a few moments, then began to soap herself all over. She had colour-polished her toenails to match her fingers, all ready for Mauritius, she thought ironically, lifting one slim foot out of the

water, and she had had her legs waxed. All this un-
accustomed body pampering for a romantic vacation which had never happened. She supposed
she should remove the bright coral varnish. It
seemed out of place at the cottage, and would soon
chip anyway.

She paused again, listening intently, aware of a
vague unease, but there was still nothing but silence
from the room above. However, she wouldn't push
her luck by staying in the tub for her usual leisurely
soak, she decided. There was supper to get, even
if it only meant heating up Mrs Grice's pie and
cooking the vegetables to go with it.

Besides, she suddenly felt uncomfortable for
some reason. Surely it couldn't just be the fact of
Jay's silent presence upstairs which was making her
feel so edgy—so overlooked. Ridiculously, she
found herself glancing up at the ceiling, checking
if there were any convenient cracks in the plaster
through which he might be watching her, but there
were not, as she knew perfectly well.

But she still wasn't going to linger, she told
herself, lifting herself gracefully out of the water
and reaching out a hand for her towel.

And saw, out of the corner of her eye, her
movement matched by another in the gathering
darkness outside the window she hadn't thought to
curtain. Saw it and recognised it as the hidden
watcher's sudden shift in position to get a better
view of her revealed nakedness.

'What . . .?' The words came out of her throat as
a scream. 'Oh, no.' She grabbed the towel, panic

making her clumsy, only to see it slither into the water.

Sobbing with fright and outrage, she sank down on her knees, trying frantically to cover herself with her hands, dragging at one of the kitchen chairs to use as a barrier—anything to prevent those eyes in the darkness seeing any more than they had already.

And heard, with incredulity, Jay's door crash open above her, the clatter of his feet coming downstairs at breakneck speed.

'What the hell's the matter?' His voice was hoarse. He stared at her crouching beside the tub. 'Have you fallen—hurt yourself?' He took a quick step towards her, and she flinched away.

'No. There's someone—out there—spying on me.' The words were torn out of her. 'I saw him move—a face at the window.'

Two strides took him to the door. He flung it open and cold, rain-washed air flooded into the room. Maggie stayed where she was, on the floor, shivering, fighting the sobs rising in her chest. He was only gone a few minutes.

'There's no one there now,' he said, as he latched the door. 'Are you certain you saw someone?'

'Quite certain.' There were shocked tears on her face, scalding her chilled flesh.

'Well, he must be a determined bastard,' Jay said grimly. 'This place is about as remote as you can get, and the weather conditions aren't ideal for playing Peeping Tom either. Have you any idea who it could be?'

I thought it was you.

She didn't have to say the words. They hung in the air, unspoken, between them, as cold and as heavy as stones, and she saw Jay's face harden into anger.

'Sorry to disappoint you,' he said harshly. 'But peering through windows, or keyholes, has never been my bag. You must have another admirer, darling.'

'Don't.' Her voice cracked.

Jay sighed, raking an exasperated hand through his hair. 'I'm sorry, but your dogged insistence that I'm some kind of pervert gets to me sometimes.' He glanced at the windows. 'If you don't like being the floorshow, perhaps you should start drawing the curtains.'

'I never thought,' she said wretchedly. 'I'm just wondering how many other times—oh, I feel sick.'

'No, you don't,' Jay said curtly. 'You've had a lousy experience, and you're shocked, but it's all over now, so there's no need to be sick or faint, or even cry any more. And he won't be back—not now he knows you've spotted him, and probably told the police.' He paused. 'So I suggest you stop trying to burrow through the flagstones, and put something on before you catch pneumonia.'

'Oh.' If she had been shivering before, she was burning now, as it occurred to her what kind of picture she was presenting. She wrapped her arms even more tightly round her body, and stared down at the floor, dying of mortification.

'Where's your towel?'

'I dropped it in the bath,' she said in a muffled voice.

'It just isn't your day, lady.' She didn't have to look at him. She could hear the grin in his voice. 'Wait there, and I'll fetch you a robe.'

She didn't think she was capable of moving. She just wanted to vanish—to dematerialise, so that she would never—ever have to face Jay Delaney again, she thought, suppressing another sob.

He was back almost at once with her robe, which he draped round her shoulders.

He said casually, 'If it's any consolation, I doubt whether Peeping Tom or I saw any more than you'd have shown on the beach on Mauritius.'

She huddled into the robe, fastening its sash with fingers that shook. 'I'm—not a very daring sunbather.'

'Then you should change your policy.' Jay filled the kettle and set it to boil. 'The more you take off, Ms Carlyle, the better you look. And I apologise for calling you "underdeveloped",' he added.

'Thank you,' Maggie said between gritted teeth. 'If this is supposed to make me feel happier about what happened, it's wide of the mark. I can do without your sexist garbage.'

He gave her an amused glance. 'Said with all your old bite. Cowering on the floor isn't your style at all, Maggie. You should have given Peeping Tom one of your looks—made his dirty mac burst into flames.'

She had not expected to smile again, but somehow, briefly and unwillingly, she did. And somehow, too, Jay had cleared the bath away, and she was sitting in the rocking chair warming her hands on a mug of coffee.

She waited until he picked up his own beaker and sat at the kitchen table with it, then said, slowly, 'Jay—I'm glad I wasn't alone here—for that.'

'You'd probably have been safe,' he said, after a pause. 'Lookers aren't always touchers.'

They are sometimes. Memories, rigorously suppressed, rose to the forefront of her mind. She clamped her teeth on the beaker to stop them chattering.

'Have you had any further thoughts on the guy's identity?'

She hesitated. 'There's a man at the farm who's a bit of a nuisance sometimes. He brought the supplies down earlier. But I wouldn't have thought...'

'No,' he said. 'It was easier to think I'd be prepared to risk life and limb shinning down some drainpipe for a quick drool. Your resident pervert.' There was real bitterness in his tone, and she looked at him in swift surprise.

She began, 'I'm sorry...' but he cut across her.

'Let's get a couple of things straight, shall we? I don't give a damn whether you believe this or not, but I did not rape Debbie Burrows. In fact, I never laid a hand on her. And I'm not going to rape you either, Ms Carlyle. If you want anything from me, lady, you're going to do the asking. You may even have to go down on your knees and beg me.'

Maggie set down her mug. 'I think you must be out of your mind,' she said hoarsely.

He shook his head. 'No, I'm not. Why don't you start being honest, Maggie—with yourself as well as with me? There's been something there from the moment we met, and you know it.'

'I think you're getting real life confused with a script from one of your television shows.' She could hear the shake in her voice, and strove to sound calm. 'Our paths have happened to cross, that's all. But as soon as the roads re-open, and we can get out of here, we'll be going our separate ways, and it can't be too soon for me.'

'Yet who can say when that happy day will be?' Jay drawled. 'I imagine clearing a way to this rustic retreat will be well down on the list of national priorities.'

She lifted her chin. 'Mr Grice knows I want to get away urgently. He won't leave me trapped here.'

'So you regard this little ivory tower of yours as a trap now? That's interesting. So where do you plan to take refuge next?'

'I have a life in London,' Maggie said with dignity. 'And a boyfriend whom you seem to have forgotten about.'

'The guy with the ailing mother?' Jay's lip curled. 'I'd say he's forgotten about you—wouldn't you? Don't rely on finding sanctuary with him. And the fact that you call him your boyfriend says a hell of a lot too. You don't need a boyfriend, Maggie. You need a man.'

'How dare you? You know nothing about Robin...'

'I know that he's started using his mother as a shield against you, either consciously or unconsciously—and with her full connivance,' Jay said flatly.

'That's not true . . .'

'Then why are you here with me, instead of Mauritius with him?'

'Naturally I was upset when our trip was cancelled,' she said coldly. 'I wanted to get away by myself for a few days—work some things out in my head.'

'So did I. Only the forces of nature screwed things up—for both of us,' Jay said mockingly. 'Now drink the rest of the coffee, and tell me what we're having for supper. I'll get it ready.'

'Use whatever food you want. I'm not hungry.' Maggie concealed the fact that her hands were trembling in the folds of her robe.

'Dishonest, and stubborn too.' Jay shook his head sadly. 'And I always understood adversity brought out the best in people.'

'Oh, leave me alone,' Maggie shot at him. 'This has been the worst twenty-four hours of my life. I missed out on my holiday, my car's been wrecked, and I've been spied on by some lecherous creep.' She swallowed an angry sob. 'And all you can do is wind me up.'

'That,' Jay said evenly, 'is all you'll allow me to do.' He discovered the pie, waiting on a work surface, and held it up. 'Do you want to eat this hot or cold?'

'I've told you. I don't want anything.'

'Tough,' Jay said pleasantly. 'I didn't let you have hysterics earlier, and I'm not allowing you to starve yourself either. You'll eat, even if I have to stuff every mouthful down your throat personally. Do I make myself clear.'

'Oh, very macho,' Maggie hurled at him furiously. 'Very Hal McGuire.'

'Wrong,' he said. 'He's fiction, and I'm fact. As a publishing lady, I'd have thought you knew the difference. And McGuire wouldn't be standing here arguing the toss with you either,' he added with a touch of grimness. 'He'd be sorting out your problems in bed, right now.'

'Sex as a panacea for all ills? Now there's an original thought.' Maggie gave a small strident laugh.

'And how would you know?' Jay's eyes met hers with steely steadiness. 'All the evidence so far suggests it's a form of treatment you've never tried, and have never been seriously tempted to try, not even with good old Robin, so don't knock it.'

'How dare you . . . ?'

'You're starting to repeat yourself, Maggie.'

'I refuse to go on with this conversation.' She got hurriedly to her feet, stumbling a little, to her annoyance, over the hem of her robe. 'I'm going to my room.'

'To dress for dinner, I hope.'

'Why should I?'

'Because we both know that you're naked under that robe, sweetheart, and before the evening's over I might find that an irresistible challenge.'

Swift colour stung at Maggie's cheeks, but she managed a scornful laugh. 'So much for your stern resolution. I thought you said I had to make the running from now on.'

'So you do,' Jay said pleasantly. 'But I don't discount a little—friendly persuasion on my part.' He turned away to adjust the oven control on the Aga. 'I'll call you when dinner's ready.'

Maggie was shaking from temper mingled with genuine alarm when she got to her room. She was sorely tempted to turn the key in the lock and defy him, but although her door was solid, its hinges had seen better days. One good push from a determined shoulder might be all that was needed, she realised with trepidation. Jay might claim that the more muscular side of his McGuire role was performed by stuntmen, but his own physique left nothing to be desired, and he was certainly determined, she thought, biting her lip.

It seemed her best course of action was to get dressed in the most anonymous and asexual set of garments she could find, and try to get through dinner with him without further arguments or major confrontations.

And, after that, start praying that deliverance would come soon.

She gave a soundless sigh, and began to rummage through her limited wardrobe. Clean jeans, she thought, and a woollen shirt, topped by a Shetland sweater that she normally wore only for gardening because it had stretched. Just let him try and find anything seductive about those.

She dressed, then brushed and divided her hair into two braids which she pinned on top of her head.

I look like hell, she decided with gloomy satisfaction.

Jay had said he would call her, but she felt it would be better to take the initiative and join him downstairs, rather than skulk about in her room, as if she were afraid of him.

When she got to the foot of the stairs she halted, staring round her in disbelief. The curtains had been drawn, music was playing softly from her small radio, and the room's only illumination came from candles glimmering on the neatly set table. Jay was standing with his back to the stove, glass in hand.

Maggie was just about to say something acid about cliché situations when it occurred to her just in time that he was waiting for precisely such a remark, and undoubtedly had his comeback prepared.

She schooled her face hurriedly to appreciation. 'How nice it all looks.'

'I'm glad you approve,' he said courteously.

'And I'm starving,' she went on brightly, for good measure.

'I wish I could offer you a drink,' he said. 'But apart from my scotch, which you don't care for, there seems to be a dearth of alcohol in this place.'

'I hardly ever drink,' Maggie said, dismissing from her mind the several bottles of wine she knew were lurking at the back of a cupboard in the cavernous dresser. She needed to keep her wits about her, unblurred.

'I always believed that gin and tonic was the lifeblood flowing through publishers' veins.'

Maggie smiled sweetly. 'We're a new company. We stick to mineral water. Anyway, gin gives me a headache.'

'And that's the last thing we want to happen,' Jay said silkily. 'Take a seat, Ms Carlyle. Your dinner is served.'

The pie was one of Mrs Grice's triumphs, Maggie had to acknowledge, and the vegetables were slightly crisp, as she liked them. There was cheese and fruit to follow, and Maggie lingered over it, eating rather more than she really wanted, trying to spin out the time.

I'll have to take ages over the washing up, she thought ruefully, but that still leaves a hell of a lot of evening to get through.

Eventually, she had to push her plate away.

'Coffee?' She half rose to her feet, but Jay gestured to her to stay put.

'I'll make it.'

'Then I'll start the washing up.'

'There's no hurry.' He pointed to the rocker beside the Aga. 'Relax for a while.'

She sat, watching him. His movements were deft and economical as he cleared the table and stacked the used dishes beside the sink, and his lean body had an instinctive animal-like grace which wasn't lost on her. For the first time, she wished the cottage was equipped with television, so that she could have another focus for her attention. As it was, there wasn't even a newspaper or a magazine she could bury herself behind.

When the coffee was brewing, Jay came to stand in front of her.

'The lack of seating round here is a distinct obstacle to the cosy domestic evening I have in mind,' he remarked. 'However, there is a simple solution.'

Before Maggie could fathom what he meant, or, indeed, take evasive action, he bent, scooped her effortlessly out of the rocking chair into his arms, then sat down in her place, depositing her on his knee.

'How dare you?' Maggie found herself struggling in vain against the imprisoning arm which held her like a band of steel. 'Let me up this instant, damn you. I should have known you couldn't be trusted...'

'I'll be perfectly trustworthy,' Jay retorted. 'Just as long as you sit still. Did your mother never warn you, Maggie Carlyle, that wriggling round on a man's lap can give him ideas?'

'No.' Her throat seemed to close over. 'Let go of me—please.'

'Why so uptight?' He showed no sign of relinquishing his grip even fractionally.

'Because I can't stand it,' she said hoarsely. 'I can't bear to be—forced.'

'And I dislike being treated as if I were unclean in some way.' He gave her a measured look. 'Face it, Maggie. There's no guarantee that this is all going to be over tomorrow. We have to learn to accept each other's presence, maybe for some time to come,' he added grimly.

'And is this how you plan to do it—by harassing me?'

He sighed. 'There's no harassment,' he said wearily. 'Good lord, even the slightest physical contact with a man seems to have you climbing the walls. I begin to feel almost sorry for the boyfriend. I'm not surprised he chickened out. What's your idea of foreplay, Maggie—six hours of grovelling?'

'You're disgusting,' she said. 'And of course your immense ego wouldn't credit that it's you I can't stand—your touch—contact with you.'

'You've made your point.' His arm tightened round her. 'But it's an allergy you're going to have to overcome, unless you want to emerge from this idyll as a gibbering wreck. Take the ramrod out of your backbone, Maggie. So, you've had a trying twenty-four hours. It hasn't been undiluted bliss for me either. Lean against me. Use my shoulder. If nothing else works, pretend I'm the boyfriend.'

If she hadn't been so upset, that could almost have been laughable. Physically, Jay and Robin were at opposite ends of the spectrum. Robin wasn't overweight particularly, but his frame was cushioned, comfortable. Jay's body, by contrast, was tough and spare, all bone and lithe muscle.

Even the scent of their skins was totally different. Robin had used the same brand of toiletries for years. The fragrance was familiar to her—all part of the man she was accustomed to. The man she loved, she thought defensively.

Whereas Jay's scent was alien—clean, warm and totally male. And in some indefinable way, dangerous.

Or was that simply because she was afraid of him? Or afraid of herself where he was concerned, she thought with sudden, terrifying insight. No that couldn't be true. It couldn't be . . .

As if trying to convince herself, Maggie made herself relax, leaning against his supporting arm, resting her shoulder against his.

'Is that better?' she enquired stiltedly.

'Marginally.' His tone was terse. 'But you could loosen up still more—starting here.' He lifted a hand and unpinned her braids.

'Don't do that.' Instantly she tensed.

'I'm sick of seeing your hair dragged back and tortured out of existence. It deserves to breathe, Maggie.' He began to unfasten her plaits running his fingers through the waving red tresses to free them completely on to her shoulders. 'That's a beginning, at least.'

She found the touch of his fingers against her scalp intensely disturbing. When she spoke, her voice was slightly breathless. 'You—you expect a great deal.'

'Actually, I expect very little. Having you treat me as a human being would be a bonus.'

'And what about the way you've behaved?' Colour rose in her face. 'Ever since I arrived, you've been impossible, and worse.'

'But my conduct is impeccable now. Why don't we consider the past buried, and get to know each other a little.'

There was beguilement in his voice. The words seemed to contain a hundred hidden promises. Maggie realised that she was weakening—warming to him—and self-contempt lanced through her.

This, she realised, must be the 'friendly persuasion' he had threatened her with. What kind of a pushover did he think she was?

She made herself shrug. 'Because there's no reason to further our acquaintance,' she said coolly. 'We're—ships that pass in the night. When we leave here, we probably won't spare each other a second thought.'

'Are you so sure of that?'

'Absolutely convinced,' Maggie said airily. 'I have my work, and you have your problems.'

'But my problems will be resolved soon. And you can't work all the time.'

'I've been giving a good imitation of it lately,' Maggie admitted ruefully.

'Then you should learn to play a little too.'

'I intended to,' she said. 'That was what Mauritius was all about.'

'Then I'm sorry it didn't happen for you. Although I still doubt whether this Robin was the right man for it to happen with.'

'I don't think much of your grammar.'

'I could say the same about your taste in men.'

'You're being unfair.'

'Let me be the judge of that.' He paused. 'But we'll change the subject, if you prefer. Tell me about yourself.'

She was taken aback. 'There—isn't much to tell.'

'That's rarely true. Are your parents still alive?'

'My mother is. She lives in Australia now, with her second husband,' said Maggie haltingly. 'I—I don't hear from her much.'

'Your choice, or hers?'

'Mutual, I suppose.' Her mouth was dry suddenly. 'My stepfather and I—didn't get along too well. It caused some—problems.'

'It's never an easy relationship.' His tone was light, almost dismissive, and she had to suppress a sigh of relief. 'Is Sebastian's wife your only sister?'

'Yes—and I have a niece as well now. She's adorable.'

Jay's brows lifted. 'Is this the feminist career woman speaking?'

'No, just a proud aunt.'

'So marriage and babies don't figure in any scenario of your own devising?'

She bit her lip. 'They might have done—once.'

'After Mauritius, you mean.' Jay whistled softly. 'You had a hell of a lot riding on that trip, Maggie Carlyle. You were actually planning on being happy ever after with this guy, without any idea if you were even sexually compatible.'

Maggie flushed. 'These things—work themselves out,' she protested. 'And—sex isn't the be-all and end-all in a relationship anyway.'

He gave her a sardonic look. 'Tell me about it.'

'I think I've told you enough.' Maggie straightened, acutely aware that she was beginning to find Jay's lap, and the shelter of his arm, only too comfortable, and comforting. 'The coffee must be ready by now.'

Jay shrugged. 'It's as good an excuse as any for running away.'

'I'm not running away.'

'But I think you are,' he said. 'And I think you have been for a very long time.'

Maggie stayed silent for a moment, her breasts rising and falling unevenly. 'Stick to McGuire,' she said curtly at last. 'The role of psychotherapist

doesn't suit you. And anyway, you have no room
to talk. You're running away yourself.'

'I'm gaining a breathing space. I never intended
it to be a life's work.' He lifted a hand and stroked
an errant lock of hair back from her cheek. The
fleeting brush of his fingers on her skin nearly made
her cry out aloud. 'So here we are, Maggie, two
refugees in the middle of nowhere. Surely we have
something to give each other?'

'I've given you a temporary roof over your head.'
Her heart was hammering so hard and so fast, it
was almost painful. 'There's nothing more. Now
let me up, please. I—I don't want coffee. and I'd
like to go to my room. This—this nonsense has gone
far enough.'

He released her so promptly it was almost an
insult.

'You see,' he said quietly. 'There's no need to
panic.'

'I am—not panicking.' Her voice was a muted
scream, as she got somewhat unsteadily to her feet.
'Nor am I a suitable case for treatment. Sort out
your own mess, Mr Delaney.'

'I intend to. And then, Maggie Carlyle, I'm going
to halt your headlong flight to very little.'

'No.' She shook her head. 'No, you won't. When
we get out of here, you won't see me—you won't
come anywhere near me again. And that's a
promise.'

'But that's where you're wrong, Maggie. Because you're going to come into my arms again,
very soon, and when you do I'm not going to let
you go. Take that thought to bed with you.'

He smiled at her, his eyes holding hers for an endless moment. She felt her lips part helplessly and her whole inner being clench with a yearning she did not know how to control. She wanted with sudden desperation to be close to him, to feel the warmth of his body against hers, to spread her hands across the muscled sweep of his shoulders, and press her mouth against the tanned column of his throat. It terrified her to know how much she wanted these things.

And it tore her apart to realise how impossible it was that she should ever have any of them.

She took a step backwards from him, and then another, walking away from him very carefully until she felt the stability of the newel post under her shaking fingers.

Jay stood, hands on hips, watching her, still smiling. He said quite gently, 'You will come to me, Maggie, and we both know it.'

Her lips shaped the word 'no' but without sound.

His mouth twisted, then, with a shrug, he walked to the table and began to pour himself some coffee.

It was as if he had deliberately snapped some chain binding them together. Suddenly, she was free to go. Free to walk up the stairs into the darkness waiting for her.

And yet, at the same time, she knew without question that she had forfeited freedom forever.

CHAPTER FIVE

IT WAS a long time before Maggie slept that night. She lay, staring into the darkness, listening to the lash of the rain on the window and the muted bluster of the wind in the chimney.

She could rationalise what was happening to her, of course. She could tell herself over and over again that Jay Delaney was a highly paid and successful actor. A sex symbol, no less. He brought a stinging, charismatic power to his television performances, so it was inevitable that, off-screen, he would pack an even more formidable punch.

But, knowing all this as she did, despising him and everything he stood for as she did, how could she let him get to her as he did?

That was the question for which she could find no answer.

She was aware of his presence all the time. She was so accustomed to solitude that every sound, every movement seemed to reverberate through the cottage. She had heard the clink of dishes as he had washed up, then, much later, his quiet footsteps on the stairs.

After that, she'd been conscious of him moving about for what seemed hours. Surely it couldn't take him that long to get ready for bed, she thought fretfully. He wore few enough clothes, for heaven's sake. Sudden warmth suffused her body at the thought. And on its heels came an unwanted image of him as she had first encountered him, sprawled tanned and naked across her bed. She could remember, she realised with shock, every lean golden line of him.

Oh, this is ridiculous, she scolded herself, turning on to her stomach, and giving the pillow a resounding blow with her fist. She had to fill her mind, her memory banks with other things.

Work, for instance. She wondered how Philip was coping with Kylie St John, and grimaced. If she had submitted to fate and gone tamely back to work, once her vacation had been cancelled, she and Jay Delaney would never have met, and she would still have her peace of mind.

As soon as I get out of here, I'll go straight back to the office, she hastily placated the unseen lords of karma. I'll nurse Kylie St John through her rewrite, line by line if that's what she wants. Only please don't make me stay here for much longer.

She found herself repeating the words like a mantra until, at last, sleep overtook her...

The sun was baking hot, and there was a smell of newly cut grass in her nostrils. She breathed it deeply and happily. Her French textbook was open in front of her, and she should have been revising, but she felt too relaxed, too somnolent. The distant sound of a lawnmower provided the perfect counterpoint.

This secluded corner of the garden had always been a suntrap, and it wasn't overlooked either, so

Maggie had taken advantage of being completely alone to sunbathe with her bikini top unfastened.

She loved the sun, she thought, wriggling luxuriously on her rug.

She remembered Louie grumbling about important exams always taking place in the summer, and generally in a heatwave. Her sister would probably be preparing for end-of-year exams herself at university.

Maggie sighed soundlessly, the brightness of the day dimming for her momentarily. She wished Louie wasn't so far away, and so busy with her new life and new friends. She needed to talk to her—to confide in her. There was no one else, because it was impossible to tell Mother...

She had tried to hint about her growing fears and anxieties in letters but obviously she hadn't expressed herself clearly enough, because Louie had misunderstood, and written back bracingly.

'I know it isn't easy for you, Mags,' she had said. 'And no one can ever take Dad's place for either of us. But Mum is happy now, and we've got to be glad for her, and try and make allowances. Anyway, you'll soon be at college yourself.'

Not soon enough, Maggie thought, a shiver running through her in spite of the day's warmth.

She had wondered time and time again whether she wasn't being over-imaginative. Whether, perhaps, Leslie Forester was uncertain himself how to play his forthcoming role as stepfather, and was being simply over-effusive in his efforts to deal with an awkward situation.

But he wasn't like that when her mother was there, Maggie thought, her nails curling into the palms of her hands. It was only when he found her on her own—and that was happening more often than she wanted, making her think that he was deliberately seeking her out.

She disliked the way he watched her all the time, the pale grey eyes staring unwinkingly at her budding breasts and slender flanks. She hated the way he took every opportunity to touch her, brushing past her in the cramped confines of the kitchen, putting his hand on her shoulder or her back as he passed her in other parts of the house. Small avuncular pats, usually, but sometimes the pressure of his fingers lingered.

Most of all she loathed his moist, full-lipped kisses, and the way they were being aimed more and more at her mouth instead of her cheek or her forehead as they had been at first.

Perhaps I'm being unfair, she thought unhappily. After all, I've never liked Leslie, not from the first time Mother brought him home and said they were getting engaged. I ought to be happy for her, and I want to be. It's not the idea of having a stepfather that repels me. It's—Leslie himself.

She picked up her textbook and stared at the printed page, but the words danced drowsily before her eyes, and after a minute or two she sighed, and pillowed her head on her folded arms. She would work doubly hard that evening to make up for this, she decided, closing her eyes.

She awoke with a start some time later, not really knowing what had disturbed her. Sleepily she turned her head, and saw a pair of plump male legs, covered in fine golden hair, standing over her. Instantly she tensed.

'So this is what young Margaret does when she's supposed to be working,' Leslie said, too jovially. 'Well, you're a sight for sore eyes, I must say.'

She made herself say evenly, 'What are you doing here? Aren't you working today, Mr Forester?'

'I had a couple of appointments cancelled, so I thought I'd take the afternoon off. I came round to see if your mother fancied a spin to the coast.'

That was a lie, Maggie thought immediately. He knew quite well that her mother had gone to London shopping. She had heard them discussing it.

She said shortly, 'Mother won't be back until teatime, in case you've forgotten. I'll tell her you called.' She wanted desperately to fasten the top of her bikini, but it was trapped under her body, and she wasn't sure whether she could free it discreetly enough.

'Oh, I think I'll hang on, and wait for her. It's pleasant here.' He sat down on the grass. He was wearing white shorts, rather too trim for his girth, and a T-shirt with the manufacturer's brand name on the pocket.

'I do have rather a lot to do, Mr Forester. I was counting on being on my own today.'

'Yes, you look busy, I must say.' He smiled at her. He had very white teeth, and he showed them a lot. 'Your back's getting red. Shall I put some oil on it for you?' He reached for the bottle.

'No, thank you.' Her voice shook a little. 'I can manage.'

'It'll be my pleasure.' He tipped some oil into his hand, and began to massage it into her bare skin.

Maggie lay, tense as whipcord, her teeth gritted, as the podgy hand kneaded and stroked the length of her spine.

'Shall I do the rest of you?' He slid a sly finger under the elasticated edge of her bikini briefs.

'No.' She bit the word.

'You don't have to be shy with me, Margaret. We're going to be friends. You're going to be my daughter.'

'No,' she said fiercely. 'You're going to marry my mother. It's hardly the same thing.'

'Well, if you want to be nit-picking.' He was silent for a moment. 'This is a nice quiet spot, I must say. Ideal for getting an all-over tan. Have you ever thought about it?'

'No, and I really should be getting indoors now. I'm going over to Janette's house. She's expecting me.'

'Oh, don't run away.' His hand was on her back again, pressing her down on to the rug, anchoring her there. 'I've been looking forward to getting together with you, Margaret, getting to know you really well. You can be a bit stand-offish at times, but I'm sure you don't mean to be.' His hand slid down and rested familiarly on her bottom.

Maggie gave a small choked cry, and twisted round, trying to slap his hand away. She realised her mistake at once.

'Well, well,' Leslie Forester said gloatingly, his eyes riveted on her bare breasts.

She snatched at her top, but he was too quick for her. His hands grabbed her shoulders, turning her, forcing her on to her back on the rug, while his knee slid between her thighs.

He said thickly, 'You know you want this, you little bitch. You girls nowadays are all the same, leading men on, showing everything you've got. I've seen the way you look at me.'

'No.' Maggie thrust at his chest with both hands. 'Let go of me. Leave me alone.'

'That's what they all say.' His voice was hoarse. 'But you'll think differently when you find out what Uncle Leslie's got for you.'

It was going to happen to her—the ultimate horror. Here in her own garden, in the sunlight, in the middle of the day. She saw the glitter of his eyes, his red face sweating with anticipation, and she began to scream, a wild animal sound filled with terror and disgust.

'Stop it.' He tried to put a hand over her mouth, and she bit it hard, and screamed again. In some fainting corner of her consciousness, she realised the lawnmower had stopped, and knew she had to go on screaming.

The sounds tore out of her, hurting her throat, straining her lungs, filling the universe.

But he was too strong for her. His hands were everywhere, trapping her, pinning her down. The more she struggled, the less she seemed able to move . . .

*   *   *

'Hush,' he was saying. 'Quiet now. You're all right.'

She opened dazed eyes. The sunlight had gone, and the garden. She was in bed, tangled in sheets and covers which had wrapped themselves round her like swaddling bands. It was dark, and Jay was bending over her, his hands on her shoulders.

'No.' She tried to fling herself away from him, panic destroying her reason.

'It's all right,' he said. 'I'm not going to hurt you. You're having a dream, that's all. Keep still, while I put the lamp on.'

'A dream?' Her voice cracked, as she began to remember. 'Oh, yes.'

Lamplight sent the shadows scurrying back into the corners, but it did not dismiss them completely. She began to shake.

'Can I get you something?' He stood beside the bed, watching her frowningly. 'A glass of water—some tea—anything?'

'No.' Her teeth chattered. 'I—I'll be all right now. I'm sorry I woke you. Please go back to bed. I'm fine.'

'You look like a ghost,' Jay told her uncompromisingly. He was wearing a towel draped round his hips, and apparently nothing else. His presence made the small room shrink even further. 'And I can see you trembling from here, lady.'

He sat down on the edge of the bed, and took her hands in his, ignoring her feeble effort to pull them away again.

'That must have been quite a nightmare,' he said conversationally. 'Would you like to talk about it?'

She shook her head, her eyes enormous. 'It's just something that happens—that comes back to me occasionally. The last time was two years ago. I thought I'd grown out of it—I really did...' She became aware she was babbling, and relapsed into silence.

'Does your doctor know about it?'

'He's very busy,' she said defensively. 'I wouldn't trouble him about anything so trivial.'

'Trivial?' Jay's brows lifted. 'Maggie, you were yelling so loudly, I thought Peeping Tom had come back with reinforcements.'

She said stiffly, 'I've already apologised for disturbing you. There's really nothing you can do.'

'Unlike your busy doctor, I could listen.'

'There's nothing to listen to either. It happens so rarely these days. It truly isn't important.'

It was important once. Years ago, just after it happened, I used to wake up night after night feeling his breath on my face, those pudgy, clammy hands fumbling at me—trying to strip me.

She shuddered convulsively, and Jay's mouth tightened.

'Your protests don't convince me, Maggie. I'm staying until you calm down.'

'But there's no need...'

'*I* need to,' he interrupted quietly, but firmly. 'Are you sure I can't make you something to drink?'

'Quite sure, and I'd rather be on my own.'

'That has a familiar ring.' He allowed her to free her hands from his, and sat back, the blue eyes surveying with a certain irony the prim lines of her Victorian-style nightgown, its lace collar buttoned to the throat. 'You don't give an inch, do you, Maggie? Not even when you're asleep.'

'This is East Anglia,' she said curtly. 'I don't dress for glamour while I'm here, but for warmth and comfort.'

'Then you're certainly achieving your aim.'

'I'm sure that isn't intended as a compliment.'

'No,' he said. 'But it's restored the light of battle to your eyes. I don't like to see you so cowed, Ginger.'

'Please don't call me that.'

'Sebastian does.'

'He's to blame for a number of things,' she said bitterly. 'Please will you go now, and leave me in peace.'

'You have a strange idea of peace. The noises you were making suggested the torment of the damned.'

'Well, it's all over now.' Maggie extended a hand. 'See, no shakes.'

'But you're still as white as a sheet, and your eyes look bruised.' Jay paused. 'Maggie, I think you should spend the rest of the night with me.'

Her lips parted on a gasp of sheer incredulity. When she could speak, 'I bet you do,' she said derisively.

'What I said earlier still applies,' he said quietly. 'But you've clearly had an unpleasant shock, and I don't think you should be alone.'

'Well, there we must differ, Mr Delaney. And I think it's contemptible to use my distress to pull a cheap trick like this.'

'I'm not trying to pull anything, lady, yourself included. You need company—comfort. How many other times did you wake up screaming and alone?'

'That's none of your concern. Stick to saving the world each week on television, and leave my personal traumas to me.'

His face tautened. 'You wouldn't turn to me for help if I was the last man on earth, would you?'

'You're learning at last.' Her breathing quickened. 'Now please get out.'

Jay shook his head. The blue eyes held hers grimly. 'I prefer my original idea,' he said, and jerked back the covers.

Maggie gave a little outraged cry, and tried to snatch at the bedspread.

'Oh for pity's sake,' Jay snapped. 'You're already wearing enough material for a fair-sized tent—and my memory isn't that bad anyway,' he added pointedly.

Colour stormed into her face. 'Swine.'

'Hardly an original concept,' he said. 'But you are under a fair amount of stress. Now, are you going to walk to the other bedroom, or am I going to carry you?'

'Neither.' Maggie's hand slid under the pillow, and emerged holding the knife she had hidden there the day before. 'I knew you couldn't be trusted—that you wouldn't be able to resist playing the great lover, so I decided to protect myself.'

'So I see.' Jay regarded the length of the blade without expression. 'One of drama's first rules says that if you produce a gun on stage it has to be used. I suppose the same applies to knives. What are you planning? To fall on the blade, crying "Death before dishonour"?'

'I intend,' Maggie said between her teeth, 'to use it on you.'

'That's what I thought.' Jay swept a hand from his throat to his hip. 'Choose your target, lady.'

She tightened her grip on the handle, staring at him. 'Aren't you even bothered?'

'That depends on how good your aim is.'

She said unevenly, 'You're laughing at me—you bastard.' Suddenly it was all too much—all the disappointment, the terrors and the shocks of the past twenty-four hours. There was nothing within her but anger and pain, and he was the focus of it all.

Her voice rose, sharp with hysteria. 'You bastard,' she repeated, and she lunged at him with the knife.

His hand shot out and grasped her wrist, not gently. 'That's enough.' His voice was grim. 'Now put the knife down, Maggie, before you cut yourself. I said—drop it.'

She gasped, the furious colour draining from her face. She looked from him to the knife in her hand with horrified incredulity, then threw it away from her with all her strength, hearing it strike the wall at the other end of the room and clatter to the floor.

For a moment, there was total silence. She could hear no sound other than her own ragged breathing. And then she covered her face with both hands and began to cry with great tearing sobs that threatened to wrench her apart.

Jay lifted her into his arms and held her there, her wet face pressed against his bare shoulder, soothing her as if she had been a child, his hand rhythmically stroking the tangle of red hair.

Slowly, as she wept, the fury and the pain began to dissolve, and there was nothing left but a vast and icy desolation.

At last she lifted her head, and looked at him through her blurred and swollen eyes.

She said, the words catching in her throat, 'I don't want to be alone any more,' and knew it was the truth.

'You don't have to be.' He rose to his feet, and walked, still holding her, into the other bedroom.

He put her gently into the bed and covered her with the quilt. As he turned away, she caught at his hand.

'Don't leave me—please.'

'I left your lamp on. I'll be back.'

'It doesn't matter. Don't go.'

He stroked the hair back from her damp forehead. 'It's all right, darling. Everything's going to be all right.'

He extinguished the light by the bed, and she felt the mattress give slightly as he came to lie beside her.

She turned to him, eagerly, desperately, pressing her slender length against him, knowing sudden impatience with the hampering folds of fabric which separated them. She lifted her hands and began to tug, clumsy with haste, at the small mother-of-pearl buttons which fastened her nightdress.

His fingers captured hers, halting them in their self-imposed task. 'Relax,' he whispered. 'There's no hurry. We've all the time in the world.'

His lips touched her softly—her forehead, her temples, her eyes, and her cheekbones. His arms cradled her, holding her to him. She spread her hand across his chest, and felt the beat of his heart, strong and very steady, pulsate under her fingers. It was a strangely reassuring rhythm, and she felt the last tensions seeping out of her at the contact.

She was surrendering, not just physically, but emotionally too, drifting on some wide, uncharted sea, but it felt good. It felt right. Nothing in the universe existed outside this room, this bed, and the man who held her so warmly and so safely.

Nothing.

She tried to tell him so, but the words wouldn't come. Everything was slipping away from her in some slow, mysterious way, and she was content to allow it. So very content, she thought with drowsy amazement.

As her eyes closed, she was smiling.

A sound like distant thunder woke her. She half sat up, staring dazedly round her. Watery sunlight was pouring through a chink in the curtains, illuminating the room.

For a moment, she felt completely disorientated, then, as she began to remember, as the events of the previous night started to crowd in on her, her heartbeat quickened painfully.

She turned her head slowly and fearfully and looked down at the pillow beside her. It wasn't imagination, or another bad dream. Jay Delaney was here, lying beside her, fast asleep.

Oh, no, Maggie moaned silently. Her hands stole up and covered her mouth as she strove desperately to recall exactly what had happened—every last detail. She had been in Jay's arms, he had been kissing her, and she had begun to feel sleepy. That was as much as she could call to mind, but was it all that had happened?

She was still wearing her nightdress, she noticed with relief, so things, surely, couldn't have gone too far. But through no fault of yours, her inconvenient memory reminded her. You wanted to take it off.

She gave a small horrified groan, then tensed as Jay stirred, muttering something restlessly. The blue eyes flickered open and focused. He stared at her for a long moment, then propped himself up on one elbow, and smiled.

'Good morning,' he said softly. 'Did you sleep well?'

She said feebly, 'I—I think so. I don't remember.'

'What an admission—your first time in bed with a man.'

She sank her teeth into her lip. 'In fact,' she went on with painful resolution, 'I can't remember much at all.' She hesitated. 'Did you—did we...?'

He gave her a look of sheer incredulity. 'Darling,' he said reproachfully. 'I realise you're a sound sleeper, but is that all my passion meant to you?'

'Don't wind me up about this—please. I have to know.' Her hands clamped together as if in prayer. 'I mean, I practically invited you...'

'And naturally, I couldn't wait to take advantage of a distraught girl at the end of her tether.' Suddenly, he wasn't smiling any more. The blue eyes were glacial. 'Oddly enough, jaded as I am, I prefer my paramours conscious. It adds that extra spice to the encounter.'

She flushed miserably. 'I'm sorry, but I'm so confused. I can't believe I've done any of this.'

'What are you accusing yourself of now? We slept together, because you needed comfort, but that's all we did. You can't be that naïve, lady. If I'd been your lover last night, your body would know about it this morning.'

She avoided his ironic glance. 'I—I suppose so.'

'I know so,' Jay said with a touch of grimness. 'For a bright lady, you can sometimes be incredibly silly.'

She was silent. For all his reassurances, her body did feel different, she thought with amazement. She felt keyed up, every nerve-ending, every cell tingling and alive in some new way. And there were sensations deep inside her she had never experienced before, a strange intense heat—a fluid melting...

Oh, lord, Maggie thought, as her throat constricted in mingled excitement and alarm. I'd better pull myself together—get out of here before I do something even more stupid.

'It's time I was getting up.' The words almost fell out. She pulled back her cuff, and looked at her watch. 'Heavens, it's almost midday.' She began to move towards the edge of the bed, but Jay reached out a long arm, and pulled her back.

'Relax,' he said. 'There's no hurry. We have all the time in the world.'

They were the words he had used to her last night, she realised, but now, in daylight, they were different—holding all kind of implications, connotations which she dared not examine too closely.

His hand touched her shoulder. She felt the pressure of his fingers through the heavy cotton as if she were naked. He cupped her chin, turning her face up to his. Smiling faintly, he brushed her parted lips with his finger.

He was going to kiss her, she thought dizzily, and if he did, if she allowed it, she would be lost.

She thought, I need a miracle.

As Jay bent towards her, she heard again the noise that had woken her. But this time she recognised it for what it was, and it wasn't distant thunder, at all, or anything to do with the weather.

She twisted away from him. 'There's someone downstairs—someone at the door.'

'They'll soon go away.' His tone was lazy, but preoccupied as well.

'I must answer it. It might be Mr Grice to say that the track is open—that we can leave.'

She tried to wriggle away, but he held her, his gaze boring deeply into hers.

'And if it is?' he asked, 'Can you tell me honestly, Maggie, that you still want me to go?'

The hammering on the door downstairs was no louder than the beating of her heart. One small word was all it would take, or maybe she would only have to shake her head...

Her mouth went dry. What was she doing? What was she even contemplating?

Angrily, she pulled away from him. 'You take altogether too much for granted, Mr Delaney. Last night I was vulnerable, and you were kind. I'm— grateful, but that's as far as it goes. Actually, I can't wait to get out of here, and back to my real life. You, of course, must do as you please.'

'Does that "real life",' he emphasised the words sarcastically, 'include the mother-ridden Robin?'

'That's my affair. And now I'm going down to speak to Mr Grice.' The floorboards were cold under bare feet. She debated whether to put on her robe, but the knocking on the door was getting fiercer by the minute, so she decided to risk answering it in her nightgown. It was, after all, more than adequate covering, she thought as she sped downstairs.

The bolt was stiff, and she called, 'Just a minute, I'm coming' as she struggled with it.

But it wasn't Mr Grice on the step, or anyone she had ever seen before. It was a tall man, hands buried in the pockets of his raincoat. He gave her a swift, surprised glance, then smiled ingratiatingly.

'Miss Carlyle, is it?' he asked. 'Miss Margaret Carlyle?'

Bewildered, she nodded, wishing she had obeyed her first instinct and put on her dressing-gown. 'Who are you? What do you want? How did you get here?'

'We have our methods.' The smile broadened. He turned to someone outside Maggie's line of vision. 'Here you are, George. She's all yours.'

A smaller man appeared at the door. Horrified, Maggie realised he was holding a camera.

'Oh, no,' she wailed, and tried to shut the door, but the tall man was too quick for her.

'No need for that, darling,' he said briskly. 'Why don't we all just co-operate? It's much the best way. Mind telling me how old you are?'

'Yes, I bloody well do mind.' Maggie found herself shaking, as she registered the flash bulb in the camera going off. 'Get away from my house and leave me in peace.'

'"World's End".' The tall man surveyed the wooden sign. 'Nice, that. Very—evocative. True as well. We had a hell of a job getting down here. Had to wait while they got that bloody great tree out of the way. That was your car, was it, the one they towed away? Anyone hurt when you crashed it?'

'Mind your own business,' Maggie bit furiously.

'But it is our business, doll.' The camera went off again. 'Anything to do with Mr Jay "McGuire" Delaney is very much our business. So how long have you known him, and how many visits has he made to this little love nest? Give us an exclusive before those other bastards get here, and we'll make it worth your while.'

'I don't know what you're talking about.'

'Don't give us that.' The tall man gave her an amused glance. 'He was seen by one of the locals. He didn't believe it the first time, so he came back to check, and then he tipped us off. Only we weren't the only ones.'

'Then I'm afraid you've been fooled,' Maggie said shortly. 'Get out, and don't come back.'

He tutted. 'Now is that nice? Why don't you ask us in for a cup of coffee, and we'll talk terms. It's going to be like a siege here very soon, but I could keep the others off your back.'

'I'm not interested in any deal with you.'

'But your friend Mr Delaney might be. Why don't we ask him?' He looked past her into the cottage, his smile widening again. 'In fact, why don't we ask him right now?'

CHAPTER SIX

MAGGIE turned, her heart sinking. Jay was standing on the stairs, his eyes glittering with rage. He had dragged on his jeans, but he was barefoot and his hair was tousled. It was obvious to anyone that he'd only just got up, she thought, as another flashbulb went off.

He said between his teeth, 'Get out of here, Alcott, and take your other vulture with you before I throw you out.'

The tall man whistled, throwing up his hands defensively. 'No rough stuff, please, Jay. After all, we're old friends. We'll make a tactical withdrawal and wait for reinforcements, while you and the girlfriend get your clothes on, and your heads together.'

He gave Maggie a long, top-to-toe survey which had her writhing inwardly. 'See you later, doll. Sorry we got you out of bed.'

She closed the door on them and tried to re-bolt it, but her hands were shaking too much, and Jay had to do it for her.

He was very white under his tan. 'How the hell did they find me here?'

'Dave Arnold—Peeping Tom—recognised you after all. It wasn't me he was spying on, I gather. It was you.' Her voice cracked. 'I was just a bonus, I suppose. Isn't that funny?'

'If it is, I'll laugh at some other time,' Jay said bleakly. 'What did you say to that creep out there? You didn't give him any personal details, I hope.'

'He knew my name already.'

Jay muttered an obscenity under his breath. 'If he knows that, he can find out the rest,' he said wearily. 'Bloody hell, this is the last thing I wanted.'

She moistened dry lips with the tip of her tongue. 'He said that there were others coming. That the track is open now.'

'I don't doubt it. Your farmer friend will have been handsomely rewarded for his efforts,' Jay said contemptuously. 'Isn't the power of the press a wonderful thing?' He shook his head. 'We'll be damned lucky not to find a television crew plus the local radio station camping outside in the next hour.'

He paused. 'We could make a run for it, of course. How well do you know these lanes? Is your car drivable?'

'They've towed it away.'

'Then we'll have to stay where we are. Try and sit them out.' Jay hesitated. 'It's likely to get pretty nasty. Jeff Alcott represents the *Sunday Examiner*, champions of the oppressed, and financial backers of Debbie Burrows. Peeping Tom couldn't have sold us to a more interested party.'

Maggie shuddered. 'You could get away,' she said, after a moment. 'You could get from the spare bedroom window on to the outhouse roof, and go across the fields. If I tell them you're gone, let them search the place if they want, they won't bother with me.'

'Not bother with you?' Jay's brows shot up. 'Are you insane, Maggie? Finding you here, for Alcott, is like having all his birthdays come at once. I can see the headlines now. "TV's McGuire in hideaway love nest with half-naked redhead."'

Maggie flushed angrily. 'That's ridiculous. I'm perfectly decent. You said yourself this nightdress was like a tent.'

'But I don't write for the tabloids,' Jay said grimly. 'Translated into *Examiner* terms, your modest shroud will be "sheer, see-through" and probably "transparent".'

Maggie wanted to stamp her foot, but remembered just in time she was barefoot. 'Oh, this is ridiculous. I'm going to talk to that man—tell him the truth.'

'You'd be wasting your breath. Alcott is only interested in half-truths, innuendo and downright lies.' Jay's voice was weary. He put a hand on her shoulder and pushed her gently towards the stairs. 'Go and get dressed while I make some breakfast.'

'How can you think about food at a time like this?'

'I function better when I'm fed. I have to consider what our best move would be.'

Upstairs in her room, Maggie put on the clothes she had been wearing the previous evening. Not even the *Sunday Examiner* could make them sexy, she thought, viewing herself with a grimace.

In spite of her protest about food, the aroma of frying bacon wafting tantalisingly up the stairs had aroused her appetite, and she ate the rashers and

fried tomatoes which Jay put in front of her without
further demur.

She was pouring herself a second cup of coffee
when someone rapped briskly at the door.

Maggie tensed, spilling some coffee on the table,
as the unseen caller rattled the handle, and pushed
against the ungiving timbers.

'Jay.' It was a voice she recognised instantly. 'Get
this bloody door open. We need to talk.'

Jay was already at the door, drawing back the
bolt. As it swung open, he said, 'We do indeed,
Sebastian.'

Sebastian stepped into the kitchen, his face set.
'I tried to get here before the mob, and warn you,'
he said. 'But I missed a turning a couple of miles
back, and found myself going in a circle. I can never
find this damned place when I need to.' He looked
at Maggie and his lips tightened. 'So it is true,' he
went on, half to himself. 'Why the hell are you here,
Ginger, instead of four thousand miles away?'

'It's a long story. And this happens to be my
house. I'm entitled to be here.'

'It would just make my job a damned sight easier
if you weren't,' Sebastian said crossly. 'If that's
coffee, I'll have some.'

'Am I supposed to feel sorry for you?' Maggie
demanded, standing her ground. 'Well, I don't. It's
all down to you that I'm in this mess. You had no
right to use my cottage without my permission.'

'If I'd asked, you'd have refused, and I felt it
was an emergency.' Sebastian spread his hands in
appeal. 'Jay needed a bolthole. You've encoun-

tered those hyenas out there. You've seen what they can be like.'

'I'm finding out more all the time,' she agreed bitterly. 'I gather I'm about to feature in the Sunday tabloids as Jay Delaney's latest floozie.'

'Floozie?' Jay froze in the act of passing Sebastian his coffee, and his lips twitched. 'Where the hell did you dig that word up from? For a publishing lady, Ms Carlyle, your vocabulary...'

'Oh, leave me alone,' Maggie shouted. 'By Monday morning I'll be lucky to have a bloody job at all, thanks to you. Through no fault of mine, I'm going to be dragged through all kinds of slime— labelled as some kind of tart. I have a career—a life. What is my boss going to think—the authors I deal with—my friends?'

Jay groaned softly. 'Maggie,' he said reaching out a hand to her.

'Don't you dare touch me.' She recoiled. 'Of course it doesn't bother you to find yourself in some sordid front-page scandal. As far as you're concerned, the only bad publicity is no publicity at all.'

'Is it?' All trace of amusement was wiped from his face. 'How little you know.'

'Look,' Seb interrupted. 'We're going to get nowhere by fighting amongst ourselves. Mags, I realise how upset you are, and heaven knows you have every reason to hate me, but if we stick together, we may be able to find some way to minimise the damage.'

'I'd like to know how.' Her body was rigid, but she was trembling inside.

'By giving them a story of our own—one that they'll have to use. By turning this whole mess to our advantage.' Seb spoke eagerly, his eyes fixed on her pale face.

'I hope,' Jay said slowly and ominously, 'that you're not about to suggest what I think...'

'What choice do we have?' Seb swung back to his sister-in-law. 'Mags, you're not going to like this, and neither is Jay, but I want you to let me tell the press that you're engaged to him—that you're going to be married.'

'No.' They spoke in forceful unison.

Seb groaned. 'Think, both of you. It could work. You've been secretly engaged for some time, but you weren't going to announce anything until Jay had finished filming the current McGuire series. Then the Debbie Burrows business blew up, and you decided, Mags, that you were going to stand publicly beside your man—proclaim your faith in him. But Jay wanted to protect you. So you brought him down here this weekend to talk him round, to make him see that your love for each other was the only thing that mattered.' He paused. 'Well?'

'Very good,' Jay said sardonically. 'I can't wait to see the film.'

Seb sighed. 'Sneer if you want to, but I tell you it will work. They'll lap it up. So, what do you say?'

Jay shrugged, his face expressionless. 'It's up to Maggie. She's the injured party in all this. She may feel that being called my fiancée is an even greater stigma than being my mistress.'

She said chokingly, 'I wouldn't marry you if...'

'If I were the last man on earth,' he completed for her, his tone derisive. 'Well, I'm not asking you, lady. This is a cover story we're inventing, not a marriage contract. It's an emergency measure, pure and simple, and when the emergency is over we both walk away. So let's decide now, yes or no, before the mob out there get impatient and start kicking the door down.'

'I know it's not ideal, Maggie,' Seb put an arm round her shoulders. 'But it's the only way I can think of to get you off the hook.'

'There must be some other way,' she said desperately. 'Couldn't we just say that Jay happened to be passing, got caught in the hurricane, and needed shelter?'

'Maggie,' her brother-in-law said gently. 'You don't "happen to pass" World's End. It's in the middle of nowhere. No one would believe that for a moment.'

'Well, tell them that he rented the place—and that I'm just the housekeeper.'

'Housekeepers,' Jay said sardonically, 'rarely answer the door in their nightgowns at noon. They'll have a field day with a cock-and-bull explanation like that.'

'In other words, I have to pretend I'm your fiancée,' she said bitterly. 'What precisely do I have to do?'

'Try and look happy, and say as little as possible,' Seb said, his tone coaxing.

Jay's face was stony. 'Tell her the truth, Seb. We won't get away with just that.' He turned to Maggie. 'I shall be expected to kiss you, Ms Carlyle, for the benefit of the photographers. It will be a long, lingering kiss, but your chastity will not be affected, because I shall act it.' He paused to allow that to sink in. 'All you need do is stand there—and try not to throw up afterwards, because that might spoil the effect.'

Less than an hour ago, she thought numbly, she had been lying in his arms, wanting his kisses so badly that she had been panicked into flight. Now, the first time his mouth touched hers, it would be in front of a crowd of reporters and photographers—and he would be acting. She told herself that she should be glad.

Her voice constricted, she said, 'I—I'll try.'

'Make it a good try,' he advised succinctly. He looked at Seb. 'Once this farce is over, I'd like a lift back to town. There's no point in staying here, now that they've found me.'

'Of course.' Seb looked at his sister-in-law. 'What about it, Ginger? Do you want to stay on here?'

'I'd rather get back—if you've got room for me.'

'Naturally, I have. It'll look better, too, if you and Jay leave together.'

'We could even hold hands in the back seat,' Jay agreed, sounding bored.

'Well, go and get your things together.' Seb was making swift notes on the back of an envelope. 'I'll issue this statement, and we'll leave as soon as they've got their pictures.' He gave Maggie a wary smile. 'Cheer up, love. Just think, by breakfast time tomorrow, you're going to be the most envied woman in Britain.'

'I can't think why,' Maggie snapped, and swept towards the stairs with her head held high.

'Well, I sure as hell won't be the most envied man,' Jay called after her. 'Do us both a favour, lady, and leave that sweater upstairs for the photo call.'

Facing the battery of cameras and questions half an hour later was one of the worst ordeals of her life. But for Jay's arm, cool and impersonal as a steel bar, round her waist, she thought she might have collapsed on to the floor, her legs were shaking so much.

She was smiling so brightly that her face was aching with the strain of it. She could feel her eyes beginning to glaze over. At the same time she had to admire the way Jay and Seb dealt with the torrent of interrogation, fielding the questions and returning answers that adroitly hedged the absolute truth.

But she could read loud and clear what the reporters were thinking. *What on earth does he see in her?*

She had reluctantly complied with Jay's request, and left the shapeless sweater on the bed. She had even, despising herself, brushed her hair and put on some make-up, but she still wouldn't set the world on fire, and she knew it.

Inevitably it became her turn to be questioned. 'Ms Carlyle.' It was Jeff Alcott speaking. 'Every woman in Britain will want to know—how did you tame Hal McGuire?'

'I don't think I have. In fact, I wouldn't dream of trying. He's fine just as he is.' Was it really herself saying the words, she wondered dazedly.

'How did he propose?' someone else called out.

'Very romantically.' Nervous wreck that she was, Maggie scented a chance for vengeance. 'It was a wonderful moonlit night, and he went down on one knee—with a bouquet of red roses.'

'You're forgetting the champagne, my sweet,' Jay said silkily, his arm tightening perceptibly round her.

'Did you drink it out of her shoe, Jay?' a reporter called, laughing.

'That's rather old-fashioned,' Jay returned. 'However, we don't intend to supply you with every intimate detail of our courtship, gentlemen.' The smile he turned on Maggie smouldered with lust, but the ice in the blue eyes warned her unequivocally not to play any more games.

A tinge of colour rose in her face as she tried hard not to consider the implications of what he had just said.

'One last question, Ms Carlyle.' Alcott again. 'How did you feel to learn that your romantic lover had been accused of rape?'

'Naturally, I was shocked—and hurt.' She felt Jay tense beside her; saw Sebastian's head come up sharply.

'You didn't consider breaking off the engagement?'

'Never.' Maggie shook her head. 'When I said I was hurt, Mr Alcott, I didn't mean on my own behalf.' She took a deep breath. 'I was hurt for Jay.

Because I know that he's never raped anyone in his life. He simply isn't capable of such a brutal act. McGuire is a violent man, but that's just a part Jay plays on television. I know the real man, and he's totally different.'

'Would you like him to give up McGuire?'

Maggie hesitated, then lifted her chin. 'Yes,' she said. 'I suppose I would.'

Jay laughed. 'You know what?' he said. 'For you, my darling, I just might do that.'

He pulled her into his arms, close against his body, looked down into her eyes for a long intense moment, then found her mouth with his.

Maggie stood, still and submissive, within the circle of his arms. She thought, 'I mustn't think about this. I've got to pretend that it isn't happening—remember he's only acting.'

But it wasn't easy. Not when even the gentlest pressure from his cool lips on hers could send a long, sweet shiver rippling through her innermost being.

But this undemanding contact was only the mimicry of passion. And suddenly, fiercely, illogically, she wanted more.

I want to be desired, she realised with amazement. I want his need for me to blot out Leslie Forester and everything that happened when I was seventeen. I don't want to be afraid any more.

Deliberately she moved closer to him, parting her lips beneath his with a little indrawn breath of acquiescence, letting her lids sweep down to veil her eyes.

She felt the sudden answering tension in his lean body, the swift response as his mouth moved on hers, savouring her, tasting her, kissing her more deeply. She sensed the hunger in him building as his tongue flickered along the softness of her lower lip, then began to explore the inner recesses of her mouth.

Acting on blind instinct, Maggie locked her hands at the back of his neck, and kissed him back, letting the tip of her tongue play with his at first, then become bolder, more demanding in turn.

Jay twisted his fingers into the shining mass of her hair, then let his other hand slide down her body to her hip, moulding its contour with blatant possessiveness as their bodies ground together. His tongue thrust against hers with a new and disturbing urgency. She felt her body, the ungiven core of her womanhood, melting, dissolving, turning to flame, and a small greedy moan rose in her throat.

Someone in the Press corps gave a faint ironic cheer, and the spell was broken in an instant. Jay tore his mouth away from hers almost angrily. His breathing was uneven, and there was a dull flush along his cheekbones.

He said quietly, 'I hope you've got all you want, gentlemen, because we're leaving now. And in future we'd appreciate a little privacy.'

'Some hopes,' Seb muttered.

Maggie could feel his gaze on her, bewildered and a little anxious. She didn't blame him. She felt totally confused herself. She had obeyed an impulse too strong to be denied, which she would probably regret for a very long time—maybe even the rest of her life.

Jay's own expression was shuttered, enigmatic. She did not, she decided, want to know what he was thinking.

They sat in the back of Seb's Jaguar, and Maggie tensed as Jay slid an arm round her shoulders, her heart fluttering wildly against her ribcage.

'Smile,' Jay directed her tersely. 'And see if you can manage a wave to the bastards.'

The car gathered speed, rounded the bend in the track, and Jay's encircling arm was withdrawn with insulting promptness.

He said grimly, 'And that's the end of that.'

He threw himself back into his corner of the seat, and stared out of the window, his face set and forbidding.

Maggie huddled in her own corner, a prey to her thoughts. She had been so afraid that she had revealed too much of herself, too much of her emotional turmoil in that long, devastating kiss, but, it seemed, it hadn't had the slightest effect on Jay. He was probably quite used to that kind of reaction from the women in his arms. Quite apart from his personal love life, which she didn't want to think about, even in passing, there were the glamorous actresses he made love to each week in his TV series. He had learned to be totally casual, completely uninvolved, but she couldn't be, she realised, thrusting her hands into her jeans pockets to hide the fact that they were trembling.

She had been shattered by that kiss, stirred to the depths of her being by the surge of sheer physical hunger it had evoked. But it meant nothing to him. He had only been acting. That was what she had to remember if she was to retain any semblance of sanity.

At last, she broke the silence between them. 'How—how long do you think we need to go on—pretending.'

'Ask Sebastian.' Jay's lip curled slightly. 'It was his idea, after all.'

'I suppose so,' she said in a subdued voice.

'I think we need to be talking months rather than weeks.' Maggie could see Seb frowning in the driving-mirror as he spoke. 'And certainly we have to see this Debbie Burrows fiasco over with and buried before there's any mention of a break-up.' He paused. 'It was good of you to—speak up for Jay, as you did. Very convincing.'

'I'm surprised she didn't choke on the words,' Jay drawled. 'She had enough to say about my general lack of morals when we first met.'

Maggie bit her lip. 'Perhaps I've—changed my mind.'

His glance was coolly indifferent. 'Please don't damage your conscience on my behalf, Ms Carlyle. It really doesn't matter.' He hesitated. 'I suppose this charade of an engagement will necessitate us appearing together in public from time to time, but I promise I'll keep such occasions to a minimum.'

'Thank you.' Her tone sounded stifled.

'Oh, but the gratitude's all on my side,' he said too courteously. 'As Seb remarked, that was an excellent performance you gave back there.'

She swallowed. 'I—hope I shan't be called on to go to such lengths again.'

'My sentiments entirely.' He gave her a brief smile which did not reach his eyes, then transferred his attention pointedly to the scenery.

Conversation thereafter was desultory, much of it initiated by Sebastian, and dealing mainly with the trail of devastation the hurricane had left. The roads they were travelling on were littered with fallen branches and other debris, and in a field they saw a number of caravans lying forlornly on their sides. Maggie was appalled to see the number of trees which had been completely uprooted. It was possible to trace the path of the storm as if some giant had walked through the countryside, sickle in hand, laying waste on either side of him.

She swallowed. She felt part of that devastation, swept up in the storm and then discarded. But what else, in all honesty, could she have expected?

She and Jay had been thrown together by sheer mischance. She had discovered that many of her preconceptions about him were wrong. She had found, for instance, that he could be kind.

For a heart-lurching moment, she remembered the sanctuary she had found in his arms the previous night, the tenderness in the lips which had briefly caressed her face.

Now he was an icy stranger, the distance between them as wide and impenetrable as a desert. Clearly their time together at World's End was something he wanted to put from his mind and his life as quickly as possible, and it had angered him that they were still bound together, even by this token lie of an engagement.

Her hands clenched together in her lap. Try as she might, she couldn't suppress the thought that if they hadn't been interrupted—if the world hadn't come knocking on the door, destroying their seclusion—things might have been very different.

Last night, she had said, 'Don't go.'

What if he had used the same words to her this morning? What if he had said, 'Don't leave me'? Would she have had the strength to resist?

Instead, she thought wretchedly, I asked for a miracle. Only it hasn't turned out quite how I expected.

But she had done the right thing—the sensible thing, she told herself. She was too raw, too inexperienced in passion and its demands to become the plaything of a man like Jay Delaney. She hadn't the sophistication which would have allowed her to amuse herself and then walk away. And that was all he would have wanted—someone to relieve the tedium of his enforced exile. It would have entertained him, no doubt, after all her protestations, to have seduced her—watched her surrender. But she might have ended up weeping inside for all eternity.

She was only thankful that she hadn't gone away with Robin, because she knew now it would have been a total disaster. He had been what she thought she wanted—what she believed she could cope with in a relationship. But she was wrong. Robin had represented safety and a kind of security, but he would never have turned her to flames in his arms.

I could have ended up hurting him very badly, she realised, and shivered a little.

'Are you cold?'

She flushed at the abrupt question. 'No, thanks. I shall just be glad when all this is over.'

'That goes for both of us.' He paused. 'You're still going to find the stories in tomorrow's papers hard to take, but there's nothing we can do about that.'

'I suppose not.' She didn't look at him.

'You're going to have to keep up the pretence,' he went on. 'Don't be tempted to tell anyone the real truth—not your best friend—not your boss.' Another silence. 'Not even Robin.'

'But I've got to give him some explanation,' she said, dismayed. 'I've been seeing him all this time and ...'

Jay shrugged cynically. 'Tell him it was love at first sight,' he said. 'That I swept you off your feet into a whirlwind romance. That will make it more believable when we tell the world in a few weeks that we made a terrible mistake. Presumably, Mother permitting, he'll still be around to pick up the pieces.'

'I can always hope,' she said lightly. 'Seb, could you drop me first, please.'

'You don't want me to come in with you?' her brother-in-law asked. 'You might get some reporters ringing up.'

'I'll switch on the answering machine. I'll be fine, honestly.'

'And besides,' Jay said softly, jeeringly. 'You prefer being on your own, don't you, Ms Carlyle?'

I want to be on my own tonight, she thought achingly. I need to get you out of my head, and my heart. To belong to myself again, somehow.

Aloud, she said, 'I'm glad I've got through to you at last, Mr Delaney.'

And after that there was silence between them.

Outside her flat, she waited in the chilly wind while Seb retrieved her case from the boot. Jay came to stand beside her.

'Goodbye, Maggie.' His smile was as perfunctory as his brief handshake. 'I'll get Seb to call you next week—arrange the obligatory date. We could have dinner, perhaps, or see a show.'

Her voice was strained. 'If we must.'

'We have no choice,' he said harshly. 'We've told the story. Now we stick to it.'

He went round and got into the front passenger seat beside Sebastian. As they drove off, he did not look back.

She picked up her case, and stood for a moment, looking at the threatening sky.

She had talked so much, she thought ironically, about her precious solitude. Now, for the first time in her life, she knew what it was to feel completely alone. And the pain of it was almost more than she could bear.

CHAPTER SEVEN

'WELL, I don't understand any of this.' Philip shook his head. 'Only last week you stood in this office and told me you were off to the Indian Ocean with Whatsisname. In fact, you were adamant about it,' he added severely. 'Then, yesterday at breakfast, all hell breaks loose. People start ringing up, asking me if I've seen newspapers I wouldn't normally have in the house.'

He spread his hands. 'And what do I find on the front page but you in a clinch with some TV star. No, not just "some",' he hastily amended. 'According to Janie and Claire, who've been weeping in their rooms ever since, "the" TV star. And you're engaged to him.'

Maggie groaned inwardly. 'I don't know how to explain,' she said lamely. 'These things—happen.'

'Do they indeed.' Philip pointed dourly at the cutting on the desk in front of him. ' "Petite red-headed Maggie spends her days in a dusty publishing office, polishing the manuscripts of such best-selling authors as bodice-ripper Kylie St John." ' He cast his eyes to heaven. 'Why on earth did you tell them that? She's bound to have seen it.'

'I didn't,' she protested wretchedly. 'It must have been Mrs Grice at the farm who told them I was in publishing. She's a devoted St John fan, so I got Kylie to sign a copy of her last novel for her.'

'Well, you can have the pleasure of explaining that to the lady when she arrives in an hour's time.' He paused. 'I presume you are here to work? You haven't come in to clear your desk, because your latest lover is flying you off to Florida Keys or somewhere?'

Maggie sighed soundlessly. 'No. I'm here to stay.'

It had probably been the worst Sunday of her life, she reflected as she went to her office. The papers had gone to town on the story, digging up details about her that she would have thought impossible in so short a space of time. And if the stories were bad, the pictures of that kiss were even worse. It was a study in passionate eroticism, and Maggie burned with shame every time she thought about it. No one who saw it would be in the least doubt that she and Jay Delaney were lovers in every sense of the word.

She had sat in the flat, slumped in despair, until the constant warbling of the telephone, before it was interrupted by the answering machine, had driven her out. Feeling paranoid in headscarf and dark glasses, she had tramped for miles, returning cold, exhausted and hungry. She'd heated some soup and made herself a cheese roll, and then sat staring at them. Eventually she'd thrown them away untouched and gone to bed. But there was no peace for her there either.

She had awoken several times in the night, the memory of Jay's warm body lying beside hers so vivid in her mind that she reached out for him.

But he wasn't there, and he never will be again, and the sooner you pull yourself together and forget everything that happened at World's End, the better, she adjured herself sternly as she sat down at her desk and pulled the folder with the day's correspondence towards her.

From their first encounter, she had been a thorn in Jay's flesh. Now she was an acute embarrassment, and nothing more, she thought painfully. His attitude had made that clear. All she had to do was remain equally aloof. It was the only course that would leave her with even the rags of her dignity and self-respect.

One of the editorial secretaries came in a while later. 'I've brought you some coffee, Miss Carlyle, and I'm to tell you Miss St John has arrived and is in Mr Munroe's office. He's asked me to remind you that you'll be joining them later, and he'll buzz you when he's ready.'

When he's poured oil on troubled waters, thought Maggie.

'Thank you, Penny.' She gave the girl a brief smile. 'I've drafted some answers to these letters if you'd like to take them.'

The girl took the file, but lingered, her eyes resting with obvious disappointment on Maggie's bare left hand. Clearly she had expected to see her wearing another version of the Koh-i-noor.

'I just wanted to say—congratulations, Miss Carlyle. We're all thrilled for you. None of us had the least idea...'

'It was all—rather sudden for me too.' Maggie forced another smile.

'My young sister's mad about him,' Penny went on. 'I suppose you wouldn't ask him for a photograph—and get him to sign it for her?'

'I'll try,' Maggie agreed without enthusiasm. 'But I don't really know when I'll be seeing him again.'

She saw by the astonishment in the other girl's face that she had said the wrong thing, and hastily made amends. 'I mean—things are rather fraught at the moment. He's still being interviewed by the police and...'

'I know,' Penny said. 'It must be awful for him. But nobody I've talked to believes a word of it. You tell him, Miss Carlyle, that all his fans are on his side.' She gave Maggie a misty look. 'I thought it was wonderful the way you stood up for him like that. That's real love.'

Maggie swallowed. 'Thank you,' she said, looking down at the litter of papers on her desk, while her throat tightened almost unbearably.

It was nearly half an hour later that Philip buzzed for her. Maggie stood up, bracing herself, then walked along the narrow corridor towards the door at its end.

As she passed the secretaries' office, Penny stuck her head out. 'There's a call just come through for you, Miss Carlyle. Do you want to take it in your own room?'

'No, I'm in a hurry. I'll deal with it here.' As Maggie took the receiver from the girl's hand, she was suddenly aware of her rapt expression and the air of barely concealed excitement from the others in the room, and realised who must be calling her.

She wished with all her heart she had opted to take the call in her own office, but it was too late now.

She said an uncompromising. 'Yes?'

'Good morning,' Jay said sardonically. 'So you survived bloody Sunday, and you still have a job. I'm glad.' He paused. 'I left a message on your machine yesterday, but you didn't return my call.'

'I—I didn't listen to any of them. I was out most of the day.' She hesitated. 'Was it important?'

'I think we need to talk,' he said. 'I'll be round at one o'clock to take you to lunch.'

'I—think I already have an appointment.'

'Then break it. Until one.' He rang off.

Maggie replaced the receiver, tight-lipped. Her only hope of retaining her sanity was to see as little as possible of Jay. She had come to that painful conclusion during her long and sleepless night. And meeting him for lunch *á deux* was just the kind of risk to her peace of mind she most needed to avoid.

'I'll tell him I couldn't break my appointment, or better still I'll nip out early, and just leave him a message,' she thought, as she made her way to Philip's office.

Kylie St John was the image of one of her own heroines, as interviewers had often remarked. A mane of dark blonde hair, tipped with gold, tumbled casually about her elegant shoulders, and her violet eyes looked at the world from under a sweep of curling lashes.

'Maggie, my dear.' Maggie felt herself enveloped by an Ysatis-scented embrace. Then Kylie stood

back and gave her a look which quivered with re-
proach. 'Philip tells me you hate the book.'

'That isn't quite true,' Maggie said, with infinite
restraint. 'I like most of it very much, but the
middle section does need a fair amount of work.'

Kylie's perfectly painted lips drooped a little.
'You mean you want a re-write.' There was a faint
note of petulance underlying her mellifluous voice.
'But, darling, you know how bad I am at revision.'

I know how lazy you are about it, Maggie returned silently. Aloud, she said, 'Of course, we
can't insist, but we've had an independent report
done and...'

'I've seen it,' said Kylie shortly. She re-seated
herself on Philip's opulently padded sofa, and
patted the cushion beside her, indicating that
Maggie should join her. 'The thing is, sweetie, I'm
totally and utterly exhausted—that book nearly destroyed me—and I'd promised myself a lovely
holiday, with no horrid work. In fact, I've rented
myself a villa in the Bahamas, and I'm planning to
fly there this week. You see the difficulty?'

'That is a problem,' Maggie agreed solemnly.
'But if you could spare a couple of hours a day,
I'm sure you could manage the re-write in no time.'

'Not without help,' said Kylie flatly.

Maggie was taken aback. 'You mean you'd want
to hire a secretary out there?' she asked dubiously.
Knowing Kylie, she was just likely to do that and
send the bill to Munroe and Craig, she thought,
sneaking a sideways look at Philip, who was looking
martyred.

'No, my dear.' Kylie gave her little silvery laugh. 'I want to borrow you. The only trouble, Philip is being the weeniest bit obstructive.'

Maggie disregarded that. 'You want to borrow me?' she repeated incredulously. 'But why—and how?'

Kylie shrugged mink-clad shoulders. 'I want you to come out to the villa with me and work on the revisions there. After all,' her tone became sugared. 'you do "polish" my manuscripts, as I read only yesterday, rather to my surprise, so, surely, it's no big deal.'

Maggie groaned inwardly. She said, 'Miss St John, I can't tell you how upset I was when I read that nonsense. Please believe me—I never said anything that could have given that impression...'

'I'm sure you didn't.' Kylie gave her a forgiving smile. 'But,' she sighed, 'it did appear, nevertheless, and you can understand why I feel I'm entitled to avail myself of your services in this emergency.'

'But, Kylie,' Philip broke in desperately. 'Maggie is officially on leave. She gave up her own time to come in to see you today.'

Kylie's eyes glinted. 'All the better,' she said sweetly. 'Wouldn't you like to spend the rest of your vacation in the Bahamas, sweetie?'

Maggie bit her lip. 'I couldn't put you to all that trouble, Miss St John. I'm sure if we spent some time together this week, before you leave...'

'But I'm leaving at once, just as soon as I can get a flight.' Kylie pressed a hand to her bosom. 'I feel as if this entire trip has been doomed, anyway.

My plane was held up by this terrible storm, then there was no electricity at the hotel for nearly two hours. And besides everything's so drab and depressing. All these fallen trees everywhere, and no one able to talk about anything but the damage that's been done. And to cap it all you don't like my book.' She smiled sadly. 'I need sunshine, and a peaceful environment. The way things are here, I can't feel creative in London. It's like living through the aftermath of some frightful bomb.'

Maggie was tempted to point out that the Bahamas also suffered from hurricanes at times, but decided it would be more prudent to remain silent.

'My dearest Kylie,' Philip tried again. 'What you ask is quite impossible. Apart from anything else, you seem to forget that Maggie has just become engaged to be married. You can't expect her to leave her fiancé at a moment's notice, and go haring off with you.'

Maggie stiffened suddenly as she took in what he was saying. Now, why hadn't she thought of that? she asked herself, marvelling. Of course, in other circumstances, the last thing she would have wanted would be to accompany Kylie anywhere, but it would be a perfect way out of her *impasse* over Jay. A couple of weeks in the Bahamas, even though she knew she would probably be slave-driven, would ease her out of this impossible situation—enable her to think straight, to get her life back under control again.

'Let's not be too hasty,' she began. 'After all, this is work, and we do need these revisions as soon as possible. Perhaps it would be the simplest answer if I went to stay with Miss St John for a while.'

If she had turned a cartwheel on the polished top of his desk, Philip could not have looked more astonished. 'But, my dear girl, your fiancé . . . Hasn't he a right to be considered in any decision?'

Maggie shrugged. 'If he was filming and had to go on location, he wouldn't ask my permission,' she retorted. 'I should have equal freedom.' She paused. 'Besides, after that remark in the newspaper, I feel I do owe Miss St John a favour.'

Kylie graciously inclined her head. 'Thank you, Maggie dear. I knew you'd see sense. So, that's settled then.' Her voice became brisker. 'Ring me at my hotel this evening and we'll discuss flight times, and any queries you may have.'

Maggie recognised that she was being dismissed for now, and rose obediently.

'Maggie——' Philip gave her a minatory look. 'I think we should discuss this further. It requires much more thought.'

'Stop trying to talk her out of it, darling.' This time the silvery laugh held a hint of steel. 'Maggie's given me her word. I've accepted it, and that's all there is to it. Now let her run away and pack her favourite bikini, while you tell me about this delicious lunch you've promised me.'

Maggie went back to her office and sank down in her chair, trembling a little. In spite of Kylie's remark about her bikini, she knew that her sojourn at the villa was not going to be an easy one. She was going to be made to pay for that remark in the *Examiner*.

But the trip would take her out of Jay's orbit, and that was what she had to remember. It was a means of escape. Desperate situations call for desperate measures, she thought.

The phone rang from reception. 'A visitor for you, Miss Carlyle.'

Maggie gave her watch a startled look. He was a good half-hour early, thus ruining her chances of taking evasive action.

I'll just have to face him, she thought, reaching for her jacket and bag. And I can tell him at the same time that I'm going to be away, perhaps for several weeks, and that as soon as I return I want the engagement called off.

But when she emerged from the lift, it wasn't Jay's tall, lean figure pacing up and down in reception. It was Robin.

She halted, her heart sinking. That served her right for not asking her visitor's identity, she thought resignedly. She lifted her chin, and walked over to him.

'Hello, Robin.'

'Is that all you've got to say?' He gave her a look of total outrage. 'You've been deceiving me—you've played me one of the dirtiest tricks a woman can do to a man—and you walk up to me with a casual "Hello". I can't believe this is happening.'

Maggie was uncomfortably aware that the receptionist was all ears.

She tried to take his arm. 'We can't talk here,' she said in a low, urgent voice. 'There's a pub across the road. Let's go and have a drink.'

Sullenly, he allowed himself to be ushered out of the building, but stopped on the pavement outside. 'Is it true?' he demanded aggressively. 'Are you really engaged to this actor?'

'Yes, it's true,' she said in a low voice. 'I wish I could explain...'

'Oh there's no need for explanations.' He gave an angry laugh. 'I've just been made to look a complete fool, that's all. I thought I knew you, Margaret, yet all the time you must have been lying to me—seeing this man behind my back—sleeping with him too, I suppose.'

'No—it isn't like that...'

'I don't want to hear about it,' he said peremptorily. 'My poor mother is completely shattered, of course, and in her precarious state of health that could be very dangerous. The photographs in yesterday's papers horrified her—she said they were like something from a pornographic film.'

Maggie's eyebrows lifted. She said coolly, 'I wasn't aware your mother was in the habit of watching blue movies.'

'Kindly don't be flippant. You've treated me very badly, Margaret, and I don't know whether I shall ever be able to forgive you. I suppose you were piqued because we had to cancel our holiday together, and you decided this other man could give you more than I could.' He shook his head. 'And Mother tells me that he's involved in some sordid scandal already. You seem to have entirely abandoned your sense of decency.'

Maggie tilted her chin. 'I'm glad to know that I've at last justified her lousy opinion of me,' she said. 'I hope the next lady who comes into your life has more luck—but I doubt it. While Mama has her claws into you, there isn't really room for anyone else,' she added dispassionately.

She couldn't believe she was saying these things, and judging by his outraged expression he couldn't believe it either. After all, this was Robin, whom she had thought she loved. For whom she had made allowances, times without number. Who she thought had broken her heart.

I crawled down to World's End to lick my wounds over this man, she reminded herself incredulously, staring at his red face and indignantly pursed lips.

But that was before the force of the gale blew Jay Delaney into my life. Before it blew away my sanity, and very nearly my self-respect.

She looked at Robin again, and sighed. Compassion dictated that she couldn't just walk away and leave him here on the pavement, gobbling like a turkey cock.

She put a hand on his sleeve. 'I'm sorry, Rob,' she said gently. 'But I'm just not the same person any more. In fact, I'm not even sure who I am.' She forced a smile. 'Keep telling yourself you've had a fortunate escape.'

She reached up and planted a swift kiss on his flushed and unresponsive cheek. 'Goodbye.'

As she turned away, she realised suddenly she was being watched. She glanced across the street, and saw Jay standing there, like a statue hands on hips. The blue eyes were narrowed, and his face was grim.

It was too late now to try and hide or plead a previous engagement, she realised. He was already on his way across the street to her.

'That was a touching scene,' he remarked as he reached her side. 'I'm only glad there weren't any photographers about. Newly engaged girls aren't supposed to be seen publicly kissing other men—or didn't you know that?' He paused. 'I presume that was Robin.'

'Of course. And a farewell peck on the cheek hardly merits an X rating.' She was glad of the excuse to glare at him.

'Is it farewell, or have you simply put the poor sod on hold for a while?'

'I don't think that's really your concern.'

He gave her a level look. 'Just as you say.' Then, 'He's not the right man for you, Maggie.'

Maggie shrugged. 'I tend to think there's no such person,' she said. 'After all, most relationships start out with ideals and end as compromise. Robin and I—had a great deal in common. We enjoyed many of the same things.'

'But did you enjoy each other?' Jay drawled, his eyes mocking. 'I'd have said that was the essential ingredient, but that it was sadly lacking in that, and in any other relationship you've had.'

'You have no right to say these things to me,' she said raggedly. 'I may be forced to pretend to be engaged to you, but that does not permit you to—analyse me in this insulting way.' She took a breath. 'Now, will you say whatever you came here to say, and then leave me in peace?'

'I'm intrigued by your notion of peace. And we're supposed to be having lunch,' he said evenly.

'I'm not obliged to take your orders either.'

'Do you wish to make a scene about it here, or shall we wait until we get to the restaurant?' His tone was too affable.

'I can't manage lunch today. I have a lot of things to do.' Out of the corner of her eye, Maggie saw Philip's driver bring the car to a halt in front of the office's double glass doors. That meant at any moment now Philip and Kylie would be coming out of the building, and they would be bound to see them, she realised with dismay. Any moment now...

She said desperately, 'In fact, I must dash...'

'Oh, no, you don't.' Deftly he captured her arm and held her. 'You spend altogether too much time running away, Maggie Carlyle. It's time you stood your ground, and came to terms with a few things.'

'Maggie, darling,' Kylie's voice cooed across the pavement, and Maggie froze. 'Is this your gorgeous man? Do introduce me.' She came over dragging a reluctant and clearly embarrassed Philip.

Stony-faced, Maggie performed the introductions. What else can go wrong? she asked herself.

'I detect a certain tension,' Kylie said sweetly, her long-lashed gaze making a leisurely inspection of every inch of Jay's lean muscularity. 'I do hope it's not my fault, but I'm so afraid it is. Philip's been so cross with me,' she added confidingly. 'And I suppose it is very selfish of me—wanting to whisk Maggie off to the Bahamas with me at a moment's notice.' She caught sight of the arrested expression on Jay's face. 'She did tell you about our plans, didn't she?'

'I think,' Jay said softly, 'that she was just building up to it. Weren't you, my sweet?'

Maggie did not meet his gaze. 'I'm accompanying Miss St John to her villa for a week or two,' she said. 'We're going to work on her latest book together.'

'But not all the time,' Kylie interjected. 'After all, Maggie's sacrificing her vacation to help me. I intend to see that she has some fun.' She paused, her smile widening. 'And I've just had the most brilliant idea.' She turned to Jay. 'Why don't you come with us?'

The earth seemed to rock beneath Maggie's feet. She said too hastily, 'Oh, no,' then flushed hotly as both Kylie and Philip turned astonished glances on her and Jay eyed her ironically.

'Why not?' Philip asked. 'I think it would be an ideal solution.'

Maggie's nails dug into the palms of her hands. 'It's very kind of you, Miss St John, but I'm coming to the Bahamas with you to work—not to have a holiday. Let's leave it like that, shall we?' She swallowed. 'Besides, Jay is extremely busy. He has all kinds of commitments . . .'

'As a matter of fact,' Jay said slowly. 'I'm as free as air for the next two months. I arranged it that way.'

She bit her lip. 'But there's that other business—Debbie Burrows—the police. They—they may not allow you to leave the country. Not if there are charges pending . . .'

'Don't tell me your faith in me is wavering, darling.' Jay's tone was sardonic. 'When I said I was free, I meant just that. The police have no further interest in me, and a statement to that effect is being issued through Seb's office. They may wish to bring charges against Miss Burrows for wasting their time, or even conspiracy, but that's up to them.' He turned to Kylie. 'I should be delighted to accept your kind invitation, Miss St John. I was going to suggest to Maggie that we take off for the sun together to celebrate my newly proclaimed innocence.' He shot Maggie a dagger glance. 'I'd thought of Mauritius,' he added silkily. 'But if Maggie prefers the Bahamas, then it's fine with me. As long as we're together, the location is unimportant.'

'It isn't fine at all,' Maggie protested angrily. 'I've said—this is a working trip, strictly business. It would be much simpler if I went on my own.'

'Don't be silly, sweetie,' Kylie purred. 'I wouldn't be cruel enough to keep your nose to the grindstone all the time. There'll be plenty of time for—relaxation.'

'You've just said my favourite word.' Jay smiled at her, then took Maggie's arm again, purposefully. 'You mustn't be such a little Puritan, darling. You know what they say about all work and no play. Now, we'd better hurry. Our table's waiting.'

Kylie pouted slightly. 'Wouldn't you like to join us instead? We're on our way to the Savoy.'

Jay's expression was rueful. 'At any other time that would be marvellous,' he said. 'But Maggie and I rather want to be alone today. I'm sure you understand.'

'I'll try.' Kylie drew her mink around her and gave him a brilliant smile. 'Anyway, there'll be plenty of time to get acquainted properly when we get to New Providence.'

As Jay drew her away, Maggie was shaking with temper.

'Damn you,' she said between her teeth.

'Smile when you say that. They're still watching us.'

'I don't care who's watching,' Maggie told him furiously. 'How dare you accept her invitation like that? Are you out of your mind? Wasn't it clear to you that I didn't want you along?'

'Clear as crystal,' said Jay coldly. 'To me and to everyone else. And not exactly the reaction one would expect from a girl madly in love. If you want to tell the world that our engagement is a sham, why not take out a full-page ad in the *Examiner*?'

'But you could have made some excuse.'

'I could, but I'd say she's a lady who enjoys publicity and knows how to manipulate it. I guarantee that tomorrow the fact that we're joining her on New Providence will be an item in more than one gossip column. And if I'd refused, or listened to your protests, it would be an even bigger item,' he added grimly.

'I don't believe you.'

'Wait and see.' They arrived at the corner. 'My car's just along here.'

'Why the hell am I allowing you to dictate to me like this?'

'Because it's all part of the pretence, sweetheart.' Jay opened the passenger door for her. 'We're going to have a champagne lunch in united, triumphant and very public bliss, for the sake of lurking photographers, to celebrate my return to unblemished respectability.'

'That,' Maggie said cuttingly, 'is hardly a phrase I'd associate with you.' She paused, as he steered the car into the traffic. 'Were you serious, then, about the charges against you being dropped?'

'I wouldn't joke about a thing like that. And may I remind you that no charges were ever brought.' His mouth tightened. 'As I told you, Maggie, I never laid a hand on that girl.'

'But she was raped.'

'She'd had sex, certainly, and she'd been roughed up a little to make it look like rape, But I was able to prove conclusively that I wasn't the guilty party.'

'How?'

'Blood tests,' he said succinctly. 'Fortunately for me, the *Examiner* had Miss Burrows medically examined immediately when she rushed to them with her tragic story.' He shot her a sideways glance. 'Well—aren't you glad to know your touching display of loyalty on Saturday wasn't misplaced?'

She shrugged. 'It hardly did much good. The police must have already known you were innocent by then.' She hesitated. 'But why should Debbie Burrows have made up a story like that?'

'For money,' said Jay laconically. 'She'd obviously discovered the kind of cash newspapers will pay for kiss-and-tell revelations and decided to get in on the act.' He paused. 'The police are having

a close look at her boyfriend. He works as a
bouncer at her club, and is known to be a heavy
gambler. He may have put her up to it.'

Maggie gulped. 'You mean that he...? Oh, but
that's horrible.'

'A lot of things in life are, which is an excellent
reason for savouring the good times when they come
around.' He slotted the car neatly into a space.
'Such as this trip to the Bahamas.'

'That,' said Maggie, teeth gritted, 'is not my idea
of a good time.'

'I can imagine,' said Jay sympathetically, as a
uniformed commissionaire opened the door to them
deferentially. 'This villa we're going to may even
have indoor sanitation, and a bath that empties
when you pull out the plug, but we'll just have to
put up with it.'

She was forced to remain silent as the head waiter
came to greet them, but as soon as they were seated
at their table and the champagne poured, she said,
'It may be a joke to you, but that cottage happens
to mean a great deal to me. It belongs to me. It's
all mine.'

'Give me time.' Jay touched his glass to hers.
'Our hours there together will probably become
some of my most cherished memories.'

'I doubt that.' She picked up the menu and tried
to focus her attention on it. 'Now that you're in
the clear,' she said constrictedly, 'there's really no
need to go on with this engagement. We could call
it off at any time. Very soon, in fact.'

'Before this Bahamas trip, to be precise,' added
Jay mockingly. 'Isn't that what you're thinking?'

He shook his head slowly. 'No way, Maggie. We stick to our original plan. Apart from anything else, we'd both look fools and attract a lot of unwelcome attention if we called the thing off so soon.' He refilled her glass. 'Besides,' he went on, 'October is the middle of the hurricane season in the Bahamas. Supposing another one blows up while you're there? I can't let you take that risk alone, Maggie. If there's a storm in the night,' his voice lowered intimately, 'I'll be there to keep you safe.'

In the silence that followed, Maggie thought she could hear every one of her pulse beats. She swallowed thickly, staring down at the printed words of the menu until they danced before her eyes.

He wasn't serious, of course. He was just deliberately teasing her because she had given him a hard time over the invitation. But in a way that made it worse.

Safe, she thought, her heart hammering. He had said he would keep her safe. But there was no safety for her anywhere near Jay Delaney. And so far, she had only skirted round the danger zone where he was concerned. She knew that now.

Her real trial would begin when they arrived together on New Providence.

'I can't pretend to be in love with him,' she thought desperately. 'So how can I possibly pretend indifference? But, somehow, for my own sake, I must. I must. Because I can never let him see—let him guess how I really feel.'

Instinct told her that to surrender to him would be to ride on the wings of the storm. But when the storm passed, all that was left in its wake was ruin. That was what she needed to remember—if she was to survive.

CHAPTER EIGHT

IT WAS sweltering at the airport. Maggie sank grate-
fully into the corner of the back seat of the car
which was to take them to Kylie's villa.

'I hope there's air-conditioning,' she said, half
to herself.

'Sybarite,' said Jay lazily. 'At World's End, you
were content with a draught under the door.'

She gave a tight-lipped smile and turned her attention to the view from the car window.

By pleading pressure of work she had managed
to evade Jay more or less successfully until the
actual time of their flight to Nassau. In the end,
Kylie had gone ahead of them by a couple of days,
'To make sure everything's ready for us all, sweetie,'
so Maggie had been faced with the problem of travelling alone with him.

But it wasn't like being alone at all, she had soon
discovered. Because he was in people's living-rooms
nearly every week, Jay was recognised everywhere
and regarded as public property. Strangers spoke
to him as if they knew him, and the demand for
autographs was unceasing. On the aircraft itself,
Maggie had been marginally amused to see how the
stewardesses fluttered round him. But she told
herself she should be glad of all the attention he
was being paid. After all, she reminded herself

firmly, it saved her having to make tongue-tied and awkward conversation with him.

However, her real ordeal was just beginning, and she knew it.

'Is this the first time you've been to Nassau?' he asked eventually, just as the silence between them was beginning to feel interminable.

She nodded. 'I haven't been abroad much at all.'

'You've never been to Australia to see your mother?'

She bit her lip. 'Actually—no.'

'Does she come back to England often?'

'Not a great deal.'

'But you must miss her.'

'Naturally. Is—is your mother still alive?'

'Very much so.' He sounded surprised. 'And Dad. They want to meet you, of course. I explained this was primarily a business trip, and was unavoidable, but they were disappointed, and insist I bring you down to meet them when we get back.'

'Oh, dear,' Maggie said guiltily. 'Do we—have to?'

'Yes, we do,' he said with faint asperity. 'Don't look so alarmed. It's only the Cotswolds you're being asked to visit—not New South Wales or Queensland.'

'Western Australia, actually.' She paused. 'I hope you won't be too bored over the next two weeks. I really have to get down to some serious work with Kylie.'

'I hope you can get her to see it that way,' said Jay with a shrug.

So do I, thought Maggie, remembering with a pang Philip's parting words to her.

'Remember, Maggie,' he had said, 'she may be one of our most successful authors, but her private life's a mess. She's been divorced twice, and had heaven knows how many affairs. She has no respect for other women's property, so I wouldn't let that fiancé of yours out of your sight.'

Then why the hell did you encourage us both to go? Maggie had wanted to shout. Instead she had summoned up a smile and promised to remember.

She wondered if Jay found Kylie attractive. She couldn't ask him, of course. If they had been lovers, she could have teased him gently about it. As it was, there were so many no-go areas in their relationship, so many gulfs it was impossible to bridge. And it was better so, she decided, concealing a faint sigh. Better not to get too close—know too much.

But if Kylie did make a play for him—if they had an affair—that would be an incontrovertible reason for breaking off the engagement. Perhaps I should throw them together, thought Maggie, wincing.

The villa was a vine-clad one-storey building, constructed in an L-shape, and painted white. As well as the obligatory swimming-pool, a path led through a grove of casuarinas to the sea, fringed by a narrow beach of pinky-white sand.

Kylie was waiting for them beside the pool, wreathed in smiles, with a tray of cool drinks to hand.

'Isn't this sheer heaven?' She stretched long tanned limbs clad in a minimal bikini. 'I'm tempted to live here permanently—buy a house—settle down.'

She probably would for a year or two, thought Maggie. Kylie had tried most of the tax havens but grown bored and moved on after a while. It seemed, from what Philip had said, to be the same with the men in her life.

Maggie felt hot and over-dressed in her slim white skirt and navy over-blouse, especially when Kylie was wearing so seductively little. Jay, she saw, was eyeing her with open appreciation.

I can't compete, thought Maggie, and I'm not even going to try.

Then why, asked the voice in her head, have you packed nearly all the gear you bought for Mauritius? And don't say it's because you didn't want it to be completely wasted.

I don't know why, Maggie told herself despondently. I don't seem to know why I do anything any more these days.

Kylie was talking about the delights of New Providence, mentioning restaurants that had been recommended to her, shops she had been advised to patronise, and bemoaning the death of limbo dancing as a tourist attraction.

'It used to make me think the most amazingly sexy thoughts,' she said, shooting an audacious look at Jay. 'What about you?'

'It made me think about slipped discs.' Jay helped himself to more ice.

'Oh, how prosaic.' Kylie pouted. 'What about you, Maggie?'

'I was wondering when you'd like to start work, Miss St John.'

'Kylie, please. No formality here. We're all friends, after all, and you're doing me the most enormous favour.' Kylie gave her a wistful smile. 'But don't let's talk about work just yet. Take a couple of days—see a few of the sights, and get acclimatised, before you force me to the grindstone.' The silvery laugh rang out.

Maggie forced an answering smile. 'Then, if you don't mind, I'd like to go and unpack.'

'Of course.' Kylie reached for a handbell which stood near the tray and summoned the housekeeper. 'Leah, will you show my guests where they're to sleep, please?'

A paved walk led from the pool area through beds of pink and gold flowering shrubs round to the side of the villa. Leah pushed open sliding patio doors and stood back to allow Maggie and Jay to precede her.

Maggie stepped into the cool shade of the interior, and halted with an indrawn breath. It was a spacious room, equipped with fitted wardrobes and units in pale polished wood. But all Maggie was really aware of were the two wider-than-average twin beds which dominated the room.

Her horrified gaze absorbed the implication, then shifted to their suitcases, standing cosily side by side in the middle of the floor.

'Pete's brought up your luggage,' Leah pointed out cheerfully. 'And that door over there's your bathroom.' She looked around her. 'I hope you have everything you need?'

'Everything's fine,' said Jay swiftly as Maggie's lips parted in instinctive protest. His fingers closed on hers in a hard, warning grip.

'If you miss anything, you just ring,' commanded Leah, and departed with a smiling flash of white teeth.

Maggie rounded on Jay, snatching her hand from his. 'What do you mean by telling her everything's fine?' Her voice shook. 'She's put us in the same damned room.'

'I'd noticed,' he said calmly. 'What's the problem? We're engaged to be married. It's taken for granted that we sleep together.'

'We aren't,' she said. 'And we don't. I can't stay here. I want to move to another room.'

'Calm down.' Jay's lips tightened. 'If you start protesting, you could make us both look like idiots. Besides, what makes you think there is another room?'

'There must be.'

He shook his head. 'Not necessarily. Judging by the overall size of the place, I'd say a master bedroom and one guest suite covers the sleeping accommodation.'

'Then I'm moving out to a hotel,' Maggie said impetuously, 'Or you can.'

'Neither of us is going anywhere,' he said grimly. 'Grow up, Maggie. It may only be one room, but there are two beds.' He paused. 'Last time we shared a roof, we only needed one.'

'Please don't remind me,' she said tautly.

'I'm tempted to remind you of a number of things.' The blue eyes rested significantly on the trembling curve of her mouth. 'But I'll control myself.' He sighed, 'For pity's sake, Maggie, how many times do I have to tell you—I don't go in for rape?'

She bit her lip. 'I—accept that. But the whole situation is impossible. Surely you see that?'

'There are certain inherent difficulties, maybe, but nothing we can't deal with.' Jay tossed his case on to one of the beds and snapped open the locks. He extracted a pair of dark blue silk pyjamas and held them up. 'Do these make you feel any better?'

'But you never wear them,' Maggie began, and paused, blushing.

'No,' he said. 'But it occurred to me this might happen, so I bought them, and I'm prepared to wear them—as a concession. If you want privacy to dress or undress, there's the bathroom. But that's as far as it goes, Maggie. I'm not moving out, or allowing you to do so either. As far as the people in this house are concerned, we are lovers who are going to be married. So we share this room, but that's all we share.' His eyes met hers steadily. 'I told you at World's End that you'd have to do the asking, lady, and that still applies.' He patted the bed. 'This is my space, and that's yours over there. And between them is an invisible line that we don't cross.' He tossed the pyjamas on to the pillow. 'And now I'm going to unpack, change, and go for a swim. Care to join me?'

She shook her head. 'I—I think I'll go for a walk in the garden.'

'Reconnoitring for a spare room?' said Jay jeeringly. 'You're going to be disappointed, Maggie. I'd bet money on it.'

To her chagrin, he was right. The villa was luxuriously appointed, but all the space had been absorbed into the existing rooms. The accommodation was for two couples only, with a flat for Leah and Pete over the garage.

So that's that, she told herself wretchedly.

She got her copy of the script and made her way to the sitting-room. In spite of Kylie's urgings, she was going to make a start on the work she had come here to do.

The sooner it's finished, the sooner I can get out of here, she told herself, biting her lip savagely.

Leah brought her a tray of iced tea, and she sat reading and making detailed notes on her suggestions for improvements until the others came up from the pool, and it was time to change for dinner.

It was an excellent meal, starting with a spicy seafood salad, going on to broiled steaks with a side dish of peas which looked and tasted like lentils, and rice. The dessert course was a guava duff, which, Kylie told them, was a local speciality.

'So, we have the evening ahead of us,' she said buoyantly as Leah served coffee. 'Why don't we go to a nightclub?'

'I'm rather tired after the flight,' Maggie said hurriedly. 'If you don't mind, I'd much rather go to bed.'

Kylie gave her a sweet smile. 'Just as you wish.' She turned to Jay. 'And what about you? Are you planning an early night too?'

'No.' Jay drained his cup. 'I'd be happy to escort you.'

Kylie clapped her hands, then looked solicitously at Maggie. 'Are you sure you don't mind, sweetie?' She laughed. 'Can you trust me with your gorgeous man?'

'She's very understanding.' Jay pushed back his chair, and walked round the table to Maggie's side. His hand stroked her hair, lifting it slightly, and she felt the pressure of his lips, swift and sensuous on the bared nape of her neck.

He said softly, 'Get some rest, darling. I'll try not to wake you when I come in.'

Kylie laughed again. 'I doubt if she'll be too grateful about that,' she said lightly. 'She looks as if she's been turned to stone as it is.' Her eyes sent a challenge across the table. 'Shall we postpone the trip until you can join us?'

'By no means.' Maggie rose to her feet. 'I'm not usually such a killjoy, but I'm just not used to long journeys. I'll—see you both tomorrow.'

The bathroom was the last word in glamour. As well as a shower cubicle, there was also a sunken bath, big enough for dual occupation, with a cushioned headrest, and a vanity unit with twin basins, running the length of one wall. There were mirrors everywhere too. As Maggie showered briefly and dried herself on one of the enormous fluffy bath sheets provided, she kept catching unexpected and unwanted glimpses of herself from various angles. Compared with Kylie's lush and pampered curves, she was definitely on the skinny side of slender, she thought, depressed, as she dropped her nightgown over her head.

She bit her lip as she regarded herself. She would have done better to have invested in some pyjamas herself, she thought. The tiny lace bodice cupped her breasts without concealing them, and the floor-length skirt was hardly more than a drift of veiling.

It was the one she had bought for her first night with Robin, she realised suddenly. Now, there was a Freudian slip. And the others she had brought weren't any more decent either.

She would have to go shopping tomorrow, she decided, although she doubted that Nassau would have much to offer in the way of Winceyette.

But at least she didn't have to endure Jay's caustic scrutiny as she crossed the room to her bed.

She was tired—her excuse had been genuine—but she couldn't sleep.

She lay, staring into the darkness, picturing Jay dancing with Kylie, their bodies moving together to some slow and romantic melody.

It was not an image she wanted to contemplate, she thought, but then neither was Jay's dark head lying only a few feet away, on the other pillow, night after night, his body outlined under the thin sheet.

She moved restlessly, her body burning. Among her contemporaries, she thought wryly, she couldn't think of one who would have hesitated for a second. They would have snatched at the moment, however transitory, and enjoyed it, then walked away, shrugging, when it was over.

But I can't be like that, she thought. I'm pathetic. I'm practically a dinosaur. But I can't give myself—casually, and pretend it doesn't matter. And I can't give myself to Jay, because it would matter all too much.

She gave a small, trembling sigh. He could not, she thought with painful detachment, want her very much, otherwise why would he have put all the onus fairly and squarely on her? *'You're going to do the asking.'* The words still rang in her head.

If she offered herself, he would probably take her, because to reject her would be cruel, and he was not, she knew, a cruel man. He had been kind to her while they were marooned together at World's End, and sometimes abrasive—and when she had needed comfort, he had provided it. But, although he had teased her sexually, spoken and acted as if he found her desirable, he had applied no real pressure. Nor had he shown any obvious difficulty in treating her with the restraint that he had promised, at the same time making it clear that he knew her resistance to him was crumbling.

'You will come to me, and we both know it.'

As if it was just a matter of time, she thought achingly. But I don't want to be—just another female body. I nearly settled for second-best with Robin. I can't do that again.

She was still awake when she heard the sound of the car returning. She turned instantly on to her side, facing the windows, away from the door, making herself relax and breathe softly and evenly.

Jay came in quietly, but she was tinglingly aware of his every movement, the rustle of his clothes as he undressed. She heard him walk round the bed, and knew that he had come to stand beside her.

He said very quietly, 'Maggie?'

It was sheer torture, lying there, pretending to be asleep, when every fibre of her being was urging her to answer him, to turn, reach out her hand, and draw him down to her.

She sank her teeth into the softness of her lower lip until she tasted blood. Until, at last, she heard him move away. And the darkness became silence. And loneliness.

It was late when she awoke the next morning, and the adjoining bed was empty. Maggie stared dazedly at her little travelling alarm clock, and sat up with a groan. So much for all her good intentions about work, she thought, as she scrambled out of bed and into her clothes.

As she left her room, she met Leah.

'You ready for breakfast now.' She beamed at her. 'You sure sleep good.'

'I must have done.' Maggie ran a distracted hand through her hair. 'Has Miss St John been asking for me?'

'No, ma'am. She's taken the car and gone into Nassau, shopping. I guess she won't be back all day.'

Maggie swallowed. 'I—see. Did Mr Delaney go with her?'

'No, he said to tell you he'd be on the beach.'

'Oh.' Maggie looked down at her plain cream shirt and slacks and sighed. Kylie clearly had no intention of working on the book today, and there was nothing more Maggie could usefully do without her.

I suppose I may as well take the day off, she decided reluctantly. But not on the beach. That would be asking for trouble. I'll stay by the pool—draw an invisible line of my own.

She breakfasted on hot rolls, coffee and fresh fruit, then changed into one of her new bikinis, patterned in black and white with a matching hip-length jacket, and went down to the pool.

It was very hot, peaceful and still, the sky an unclouded blue. Maggie stretched herself out on a lounger in the shade of an umbrella. Presently, she would go for a swim, but for the moment it was good to relax and recover from her restless night, she thought, turning on to her tummy, and pillowing her head on her folded arms.

Tonight she would have to pin Kylie down, set some kind of timetable for the alterations, or the days would just drift past and little would be done. Once Kylie had started, her innate professionalism would take over, Maggie knew. The hardest part would be forcing her to the word processor.

Maggie had been tempted to bring some other scripts from the office to work on, but Philip had refused point blank to allow this.

'You'll have enough to do with Kylie,' he said bluntly. 'And this is supposed to be your vacation as well. Your fiancé will expect to have what's left of your time.'

She had bought a selection of the latest paperbacks at the airport, but she wasn't in the mood to begin any of them yet. She was still too keyed up—too work-orientated to lose herself in a novel. She

would only start analysing—editing, and that wasn't
the idea at all.

She found her thoughts beginning to drift
drowsily, and decided to let it happen. After all,
she hadn't slept properly for days. It was little
wonder the long flight and the change of environment had knocked her out. Her eyelids felt as if
they had lead weights attached, and it was just too
much effort to keep them open. In fact, she wasn't
even going to try...

The sun was baking hot, and she could smell newly
cut grass. It was as if an alarm had been triggered
in her head, and she moved restlessly, anxiously.

I'm dreaming, she told herself. This is only a
dream. It isn't happening. It's—only a dream.

But the first drops of oil, cool on her warm skin,
were only too real—and the hand touching her—
smoothing the length of her spine.

She screamed hysterically, her body jack-knifing,
as she turned on her assailant, striking out at him,
her nails ripping at his shoulders and chest.

He swore violently, seizing both her slender wrists
in a punishing grip, pushing her down on the
lounger and holding her there helpless.

'Are you crazy?' he demanded furiously. 'What
the hell's the matter with you? I was only putting
some oil on you, for Pete's sake. The sun's moved
round. You were beginning to burn up.'

She looked up dazedly into Jay's angry face.

'You,' she said chokingly. 'It's you.'

'Who did you think it was?'

'Leslie,' she said hoarsely. 'My—stepfather.'

Jay released her, and she sat up, covering her face with her hands.

'No.' His voice was quiet but inexorable. 'Don't hide away. Is this the dream that you have?'

She nodded.

'I want to hear about it.' He took her hands away from her face. 'I think you owe me that.'

Horrified, she looked where he was indicating. Saw the weals her desperate nails had left. One of them was bleeding slightly.

'I'm sorry.' A tear trickled slowly down her cheek, then another. 'I'm so sorry.'

'Tell me the dream.' He sat down beside her. 'Tell me all of it. How does it begin?'

'I'm in the garden. It's—very hot. Someone's mowing a lawn. I can smell the grass.' The words came slowly and painfully.

'This Leslie?'

'No—the next-door neighbour, Mr Halloran. He heard me screaming—and he came to help.'

'What made you scream, Maggie?'

'It was Leslie. I thought he was at work—really I did. That's why I'd undone my top. I wasn't lying. I wasn't leading him on deliberately. I didn't know he was coming to the house. It wasn't true.' She was shaking so hard that her whole body was juddering.

Jay picked her up in his arms, and sat, cradling her across his thighs.

'No,' he said. 'Of course it wasn't true.'

'My mother said it was. She didn't believe me.' Her voice sounded breathless and very young. 'She—she was angry with me. So angry. She said

I was out to make trouble between them. That she'd seen me—displaying myself—trying to catch his eye. She said Mr Halloran had told her that when he found me I was practically naked. That it must have been on purpose.'

She took a deep, sobbing breath. 'It wasn't true. But no one believed me. No one's ever believed me.'

'I believe you. What did Leslie do?'

'He put suntan lotion on my back,' she said with a gasp, and Jay winced. 'I—I didn't want him to. I hated him. I was afraid of him. I always had been, though I didn't know why. But when he started touching me—I knew.'

'Where did he touch you, baby?'

'Here,' she said. 'And—here. And then he tried—he wanted to...' Her voice broke.

'Hush,' he said. 'Did he get what he wanted?'

'No, because I bit him and screamed, and Mr Halloran heard me, and came to see what was wrong. I thought he believed me, but Leslie told him later that I'd been encouraging him, and then made a fuss. He told Mother the same—that I'd taken my top off and asked him to put oil on me. He said that he'd—lost control for a moment, and he was terribly ashamed. He said I was a little tease, and that I'd come to a bad end. He—apologised to her, and asked her to forgive him.'

'And your mother believed that?'

She nodded. 'She loved him, you see. She was going to marry him. She'd been very lonely since Daddy... She hated me for spoiling things.'

'Did she tell you so?' Jay stroked her hair, gently.

'Not in words. But she was—different with me. She avoided me—she didn't tell me things any more—or kiss me. And she made me apologise to Leslie.'

'Dear heaven,' he said.

'Was it my fault? Even Louie seemed to think so, although she was kind about it.' Maggie swallowed. 'I—I didn't go to the wedding. I couldn't.'

'No,' he said. 'Why should you?' There was silence, then he said, 'I'm beginning to understand quite a few things now—why you were so antagonistic to me when we first met, for one. And Robin, for another.'

'He made me feel—safe. He didn't—make demands.'

'I'm sure he didn't,' Jay agreed drily. 'I'd say he had his own hang-ups to cope with.'

Maggie suddenly realised how closely he was holding her, her head pillowed on his shoulder, his hand resting on her thigh. She tried to sit up, and he let her go immediately. She sat on the lounger, a few inches apart from him.

She pushed her hair back from her wet face, not looking at him. 'I didn't mean to tell you all this,' she said. 'I didn't mean to tell anyone else, ever.'

'Not Robin?'

'No—never. I—I just wanted to—blot the whole thing out.'

'But it didn't work. Hence the nightmares.' He put a finger under her chin, and tilted her face towards him. 'Know something, Maggie Carlyle? I'm willing to bet a year's earnings that you'll never have that nightmare again.'

He bent and picked up the bottle of sun oil, lying on its side on the tiles at their feet. He weighed it in his hand for a minute, his face enigmatic. Then he looked at her.

'Let's try an experiment.'

'I—don't think I can.'

'And I think you must.' He watched her steadily. 'Trust me, Maggie.'

She gave a little shaken sigh. 'All right.' She lay down again, closing her eyes, waiting rigidly.

She felt the first cool drops of oil on her back and bit her lip, trying not to flinch.

His hands were warm and very gentle. He began with her shoulders, his fingers barely brushing her skin, anointing her with the scented lotion. Gradually, imperceptibly she began to relax under the impersonality of his touch. When he reached the barrier of her bikini top, he hesitated, then, feeling her tense swiftly, skipped over it to the lower part of her back.

Maggie buried her face in the cushions of the lounger, not knowing whether to be glad or sorry.

His fingers were firmer now, surer as they stroked the oil into her flesh, and although she was still nervous, she could feel, incredibly, her skin beginning to tingle with excitement in response to his touch.

She wanted this slow, lingering contact to go on forever. She wanted...

'There.' His tone was brisk. 'Was that too unbearable?'

She sat up slowly, keeping her flushed face averted.

'No—you were right. Thank you.'

'Any time.' He paused. 'I think I'll go for a swim. Why don't you come down to the beach and join me? There's a delicious breeze.'

'I—I like it here.' The defensiveness in her tone was unmistakable.

There was a pause, then he shrugged, his voice hardening slightly. 'As you please.'

She watched his tall figure stride away down the path between the casuarinas and disappear.

Then she lay down again, with a little tremulous sigh. Jay might have dispelled one nightmare for her, but now she had another to face.

The misery, she thought, the darkness of her life—her future—without him, when eventually he walked away from her for good. Because that, she was beginning to realise, would be the greatest nightmare of all.

CHAPTER NINE

MAGGIE put down the page of typescript and breathed a sigh of sheer relief.

It was done. It was all over, and she could go home.

In fact, she thought, there had been no real need for her to come here in the first place. All she had had to do was give Kylie her notes and nag her into beginning the revisions. Once Kylie had stopped grumbling and started working she had taken fire, and there had been no holding her.

But it wasn't just enthusiasm for the book which had been driving her, Maggie had to acknowledge, flinching inwardly. Jay's company had been a far more effective spur.

When Kylie had finished her day's working stint the rest of her time had been spent quite openly with Jay, swimming, sunbathing, exploring the island by car, golfing and playing tennis. They had even had a couple of days deep-sea fishing together. And in the evenings, after dinner, they were to be found at nightclubs or discotheques.

Maggie had always been urged to join them on these expeditions, it was true, but she had invariably made some excuse, ignoring Jay's ironic stare, protesting that such energetic pursuits were not her idea of a holiday and she preferred to stay by the pool or have an early night.

It might hurt, here and now, to know that he and Kylie were together, but it would be infinitely less painful in the long term than seeking his company herself. She knew that, because she kept telling herself so at regular intervals during the long lonely afternoons and nights.

When he came back to their room, usually some time in the small hours, she still pretended to be asleep. She sometimes thought she had turned pretence into an art form, although she couldn't be sure how good the deception was. He still came and stood for a few minutes beside her bed each night, she knew. Perhaps he was waiting for her to have another nightmare, or perhaps he was listening to her breathing. Certainly she had been the target for a few edged and sardonic remarks about the soundness of her slumbers on the rare occasions whey they'd been alone together.

She had to admit, however, that Jay had been punctilious over allowing her all the privacy she could possibly want. There had been few of the awkward moments she'd dreaded.

She sighed, and shuffled the pages of script into a neat pile, securing them with a rubber band. That was hardly to be wondered at, of course. After pouring her heart out to him like that about the dream, he probably regarded her as some kind of basket case.

Once, and only once, thinking he was already on his way into Nassau with Kylie, Maggie had emerged from the bathroom in one of her sheer and sexy nightgowns and found him there. For a moment, he'd stood there as if turned to stone, his

eyes like a blue flame as they travelled over her—
then, as she grabbed for her robe, he'd turned away
with a muttered word of apology.

She stood up, picking up the script. She would
put this safely away and maybe begin her packing.
And then, she thought, giving the garden, shim-
mering in the midday heat, a wistful glance, she
would go for a last swim.

It was an hour later that she finally made her
way down to the pool. She was so used to having
it to herself that she checked with a start of real
surprise on finding Jay there, reading.

Her reaction wasn't lost on him, and his brows
snapped together.

'Would you like me to leave?'

She smiled nervously. 'Of course not. As a matter
of fact, I wanted to talk to you.'

For a heady moment, she let her eyes devour him.
He was wearing nothing but brief swimming-trunks,
and the marks she had made on his skin were still
faintly visible. She wondered, with a pang, whether
Kylie had ever noticed them and demanded an explanation, and, if so, what he had said to her.

'I'm duly honoured,' Jay said after a pause.
'What did you want to discuss? The imminent ter-
mination of our supposed engagement?'

Maggie swallowed. 'Among—other things. I've—
finished here, so I thought I'd catch the next
available flight.' She paused. 'Will—will you be
staying on?'

It was the hardest question she had ever had to
ask.

He nodded. 'I thought I would.'

'That's—what I thought too.'

'Do you have any objections?'

'Of course not,' She forced a smile. 'How—how could I?' She tore her eyes from his face, and looked at the book he was holding. 'Isn't that one of Kylie's?'

'It is indeed. She's a good story-teller. I'm very impressed.'

'Her sales figures are even more impressive.'

'In fact, she's a fairly stunning woman altogether. She knows what she wants, and she goes straight for it. Won't take no for an answer.' He tapped the page with his finger. 'Apparently I remind her of the hero of this, Scott Maxwell.'

'I've seen so much of her work, I tend to get the characters confused.'

It wasn't the truth. No one who had read *The Midnight Hour* would ever forget Scott Maxwell, she thought. He was probably the reason the book had never been out of print. He was every woman's dream man, rich, sexy and impossibly attractive. And the love scenes between him and Victoria, the heroine, had been among the most erotic Maggie had ever read.

She wondered if Kylie was speaking from experience, and bitter pain slashed at her.

'But you should be flattered,' she went on, too brightly. 'That's one of her most successful books.' She glanced round. 'Where is Kylie, anyway?'

'She's having lunch at Lyford Cay with some people she met last night. I thought I'd leave her to it.' He paused. 'About this engagement—it might be better if you waited till I came back to England before making any announcement. I'm more used to handling the Press than you are, and they're bound to ask awkward questions.'

Maggie looked down at the tiles. 'I'd rather get it over with, if you don't mind. Seb can make the announcement for me, and I can—keep out of the way for a while. I—I thought I'd spend the rest of my vacation time in New York with Louie and the baby. That should do the trick.'

'You've got it all worked out, haven't you?' Jay closed the book with a snap, and tossed it on to the lounger beside him.

'We have to be—practical.'

'By all means,' he said shortly. 'Tell them what the hell you want.'

'That's settled then.' Maggie slipped off the flowered shirt she was wearing over her bikini. As Jay watched unsmilingly, she took the padded mattress from one of the loungers and spread it on the tiles, then sat down, and began to apply sun oil to her shoulders and arms. She took her time over it, aware of the trembling excitement beginning to build inside her under his unwinking regard.

She applied the glistening oil to the tops of her breasts and skimmed over the flatness of her stomach, aware in the vibrating silence of his sudden intake of breath. She tipped oil into her cupped hands and ran them over her slender thighs and down her long legs to the tips of her toes. When she had finished, she looked at him and held out the bottle.

'You said—any time,' she reminded him, keeping her voice steady with an immense effort. 'Would you—oil my back please?'

There was a palpable hesitation before Jay took the bottle and knelt beside her. Maggie turned on to her stomach, and closed her eyes.

This was madness, and she knew it. But, dear heavens, the memory of his touch was so little to take away with her out of the sunlight into the dark and the loneliness without him.

Let me have these few moments, she prayed. I'll ask for nothing more.

His fingers pressed into her skin with delicate circling movements, and she turned her head into the cushion with a little pleasurable sigh. From the nape of her neck to the tips of her shoulders and in to the sensitive column of her spine, his hands soothed and stroked. Every cell in her body seemed to be glowing, and a delicious lassitude was spreading through her. She felt as weak as if she had been new born, but at the same time never more alive.

'You've actually relaxed.' There was a curious note in his voice.

'I'm cured,' she said. 'Thanks to you.'

'I wonder.' His hands reached the fastening of her bikini. She felt him pull gently at the strings and then brush the scraps of material away from her body. His hands glided without restriction the whole length of her back to the line of her briefs, his touch an unashamed caress, overtly sensual. 'How cured are you?'

Slowly she turned. She lay on her back, looking up at him, and her hand went up to touch his face. She said huskily, 'Completely.'

He said her name, half under his breath, on a shaken note of disbelief, then bent his head and took her mouth with his. His lips played with hers as he outlined their parted fulness with his tongue, then gently tugged at the softness of her lower lip with his teeth.

His hand lifted and cupped one small bare breast, his fingers stroking the urgent, hardening nipple until she moaned into his mouth with excitement.

The thrust of his tongue against hers was suddenly fierce, almost savage, as if the sound she had made had tipped him over some edge of restraint, and she responded passionately, with total abandon, the last remnants of sanity slipping away, as she felt the length of his aroused body pressing her down into the cushions.

They clung to each other, exchanging kiss for heated kiss, until at last Jay lifted his head and looked down at her face, the blue eyes brilliant, the skin taut over his cheekbones.

He bent again, and his mouth caressed her arched throat and moved downwards to her eager breasts. She gasped aloud as his lips found first one erect peak and then the other, tugging at them softly, before tormenting them with the subtle friction of his tongue. Pleasure lanced through her.

She lifted her hips, arching them invitingly against his, and his hands slid down her body, sweeping away her bikini briefs in one swift movement.

He kissed her mouth, and his hand touched, moulded the soft mound of her womanhood with new and devastating gentleness. Her mouth was dry suddenly, and she was almost afraid of the intimacy he was demanding. But the warm coaxing of his lips and hands were irresistible, and with a sigh she parted her thighs, allowing him access to the warm and silken moisture of her that he sought.

The sun was dazzling on her closed lids, and its heat was all around her. Inside her, too, like a slow fire, scorching her with its sheer intensity.

His tongue, moving delicately against hers, echoed the sweet arousing play of his fingers, as he found the tiny centre of her pleasure and lingered there, teaching her slowly the meaning of this new experience. Then—caressing, tantalising, driving her slowly but inexorably towards some undreamed-of brink.

Her body moved restlessly, feverishly against his hand, searching, blindly seeking. Suddenly, she couldn't breathe, or think. Her whole being was concentrated in astonished delight on the first sharp ripples of sensation within her. The ripples became a wave, then a tide of pulsation, half pain, half rapture, and she cried out, burying her face in his shoulder as she was caught and carried away on the agonised, voluptuous flood of feeling.

As it slowly began to ebb, she opened dazed eyes and looked at him in wonder.

It had been beautiful—indescribable—yet, at the same time, it wasn't enough. She wanted to know it all—to experience the strength and power of his maleness inside her.

She lifted languorous hands to touch him, to make him aware, without words, of her need—her desire.

And tensed in shock, in negation, as he almost flung himself away from her.

'No.' The word was ground out of his throat. 'That's as far as we go.'

She sat up, putting a hand on his sweat-dampened shoulder. 'Jay?'

'Just leave it, Maggie.' His breathing was ragged, and he didn't look at her.

'I—I don't understand.' She pressed her lips to his unresponsive back. 'You said—you told me that I'd have to do the asking. Oh, darling, I'm asking now—I'm begging you, please...'

'I had no right to say any such thing.' His voice was harsh. 'And I had no right to make love to you in any way at all. Because it's too late. It's over—finished with. You know that as well as I do. We don't need more bloody complications.' He reached for her discarded shirt and tossed it to her, over his shoulder. 'Put this on.'

She obeyed, her hands shaking. Suddenly her nakedness, the intimacy they had shared, seemed a shameful thing.

She said hoarsely, 'Then why—why did you...?'

'Because I wanted to touch you,' he said bleakly. 'I also told you that once, I believe. And having started—touching you—I couldn't stop. I had to...' He stopped, his mouth tightening.

'And what I want,' she said desperately. 'Doesn't that matter at all?'

'You want to go home,' he said. 'And I want to stay. That's what it comes down to in the end. The parting of the ways—two separate lives.' He paused. 'Do I have to put it more bluntly?'

There was a devil prompting her. 'Are you—Kylie's lover?'

'Not yet,' he said after a pause.

The words were like knives, piercing her. Feeling sick, she bent and retrieved her bikini from the floor, then got to her feet.

'Then there's really no more to be said.'

'Unless you want me to say I'm sorry.'

'The ultimate insult?' She shook her head. 'No, thanks.' She took a deep breath. 'The book's finished, so there's no need for me to hang round here, waiting for a flight. I'll find a room in Nassau. Tell—tell Kylie what you please.'

She walked away from him up the path to the house, her head high. This was the last time she would have to pretend to him. She thought. The last, and the most difficult, because she was having to pretend that her heart wasn't broken.

But it is, she thought, as desolation caught her by the throat. It is...

'Now then,' said Mrs Grice. 'Are you sure you've got everything you need?' She gave Maggie a concerned look. 'You look awfully peaky, dear, for someone who's been to the Bahamas.'

'I'm fine,' Maggie assured her steadily. 'And you're very kind, Mrs Grice. You must let me write you a cheque for all this food.' She hesitated. 'I forgot to pay you for the last lot as well.'

'Well, you did leave in rather a hurry,' Mrs Grice said comfortably. She pursed her lips. 'Nor were you the only one. That Dave Arnold up and packed his things too that same day, and went off without a minute's notice to my Frank.' She snorted. 'Too much clearing up after the storm, and real hard work for him, I dare say. I never did take to him.'

'Nor me,' said Maggie with total sincerity. She paid Mrs Grice for the food and saw her off, waving from the doorway with a determined smile. When the door was closed, she almost sagged against it, fighting back the tears which had been threatening to overwhelm her for the past two days.

She had managed to get a flight without too much difficulty, and had spent the night at an airport hotel. The next day, she had taken the manuscript straight to the office. Philip had been in a meeting, so she had left the script with his secretary with the bald message that she would be away for the next week.

She dumped her case at the flat, and rang the garage where her car was being repaired to learn that it was ready for collection. Then she filled a suitcase and rang the farm to warn Mrs Grice that she was on her way.

The Grices were pleased to see her, but clearly disappointed that she was alone.

'Fancy that Hal McGuire being on the doorstep, so to speak, and me not knowing,' Mrs Grice had marvelled. 'You never let on you knew him.'

Maggie had forced herself to smile and return some non-committal answer.

Now, she was thankful to be alone. The cottage seemed to enfold her, comforting her. She put the kettle on, and went upstairs. She stood in the bedroom doorway for a long time, staring at the bed, and remembering.

'I can't sleep there,' she thought. 'Not yet. I'll use the other room. There are fewer memories there.'

Mrs Grice had stocked her with enough provisions for a siege yet again, but she wasn't hungry. She made some strong black coffee when the kettle boiled, and sat in the rocking chair, sipping it, and staring into space with empty eyes.

Every time she thought of Jay, there was pain. And it wasn't just mental anguish either, she realised. Her body, awakened sexually for the first time in her life, ached in frustration.

'I'm a mess,' she said bitterly, and aloud.

She tried hard not to think of him, of course, but it was impossible. Even here at World's End, her sanctuary, everything conspired to remind her of his presence.

Coming down here had been an impulse. She'd had the phone in her hand to call Louie in New York when she had suddenly made up her mind that it was here or nowhere.

If she was to exorcise Jay permanently from her mind, maybe this was where she had to begin. Where her love for him had begun.

She put down the beaker with extreme care, and began to weep, soundlessly and hopelessly until there were no tears left. She filled a hot water bottle and went upstairs to the small bedroom, where she lay clasping it in her arms to counteract the chill of the sheets.

She had been a fool, and more than a fool. She had bared herself to him, body and soul, and been rejected. Now, she had to live with the humiliation of that forever.

And he was with Kylie, she thought, savaging her lower lip with her teeth.

'Not yet' he'd said when she had asked if he was her lover. But he would be by now, especially if Kylie had anything to do with it. Maybe he was even set to become her third husband.

A woman who knows what she wants and goes for it, he had called her, admiringly.

I tried to do the same, she thought wretchedly, and look where it got me.

She wondered how much older than him Kylie was, and chided herself for being a bitch. Perhaps when you were as glamorous and successful and sophisticated as Kylie St John age didn't matter particularly.

She had hardly slept for the past two nights, and it didn't look as if the pattern was going to change for the foreseeable future. What did it matter if she ended up with shadows like bruises under her eyes anyway? There was no one to see but herself.

In the end, she managed to doze for a while, then woke with a start.

The door, she thought. I forgot to bolt the door.

She had got warm at last, and the prospect of going downstairs again was not an attractive one, but it had to be done. Mrs Grice might have assured her that Dave Arnold had gone, but she couldn't rid herself of the thought that he might be lurking somewhere in the neighbourhood, waiting for her to come back.

Reluctantly, she swung her bare feet to the floor and started downstairs.

As soon as she reached the bottom stair, she realised something was wrong. There was a draught of air, cold and direct as an icicle, blowing towards her across the living-room. She stared across at the door and saw with shock that it was open.

It must have blown off the latch, she thought. Then saw that it was opening slowly and deliberately towards her.

She tried to scream, but no sound would come.

He stepped into the kitchen, and stopped dead, looking across at her as she stood, a ghost in a white nightgown, her hand to her paralysed throat.

He said, 'I suppose I should have knocked, but when I tried the door, it was open. I'm—sorry if I frightened you.' He paused. 'May I put on the light?'

She nodded, and he touched the switch, illuminating the room.

'Were you asleep? Did I disturb you?' He studied her frowningly. 'It took me longer to get here than I'd planned.'

'Why are you here?' The voice she found emerged as a croak.

'I came to see you—to talk.'

'We—said everything.'

'Did we?' He paused. 'You didn't tell Seb we'd broken off our engagement. He said he hadn't heard from you.'

'I—thought I'd ring him in a day or two.'

He shook his head. 'There's no need.' He reached inside his jacket, and took out a folded paper. 'There's a press release here I want you to see.'

'It doesn't matter.' She didn't want to see it in black and white—the ruin of every dream of hope and happiness she had ever had. 'Say whatever you like, and I'll go along with it.'

His face tautened. 'Maggie—read it, please.'

She came slowly towards him and took the paper. 'McGuire to become bestseller,' she read aloud. She looked at him. 'What does it mean?'

'Keep reading.' Jay hitched forward one of the kitchen chairs and sat down. He looked incredibly weary.

> Independent film producer Sol Ebelstein announced today the teaming of top TV actor Jay "Hal McGuire" Delaney with best-selling novelist Kylie St John.

Maggie winced, but made herself read on.

> Shooting will start soon on a film of *The Midnight Hour*, Miss St John's sexy block-buster, with Jay Delaney playing the lead as Scott Maxwell.
>
> The deal was struck over dinner in Nassau this week. The Ebelsteins were staying at the luxury Lyford Cay resort, where they enter-tained Miss St John and her house-guest Jay Delaney, who was escorting his editor-fiancée Margaret Carlyle.
>
> Said Sol: 'My wife loves that book, and she

never misses an episode of *McGuire*. She says put the two together and we have a winner, and Gloria is never wrong.

'I'm really excited about the project, and I'll be in London to sign the contracts in a couple of days.'

Maggie put the paper down. 'What does it mean?'

'Maggie, you can read,' he said patiently. 'It means I'm going to make a film of *The Midnight Hour*. I told you Kylie said I reminded her of Scott Maxwell. Well, she buttonholed Gloria Ebelstein whom she knows slightly at this nightclub we were at, and told her the same thing. They went into a huddle, and Gloria got very excited and agreed to sell the idea to Sol. Apparently, he's putty in her hands,' he added drily.

'The three of them had lunch together, and thrashed out the details. Then they called my agent, and talked about dates, and money.' He pointed at the paper. 'The rest you know.'

'But I don't know why you're here. Why aren't you still on New Providence, celebrating?' *With Kylie.*

'I told you. I needed to see you—talk to you.'

'Oh, I see.' She looked down at the release. 'You don't want the news of our broken engagement to coincide with this, I suppose. Well, it doesn't matter. Handle it any way you want. There was no need to come all this way just to tell me this.'

'If I handle it the way I want,' he said slowly, 'I shall say we've set the date for our wedding.'

The paper fluttered from her fingers. She took a step backwards. 'You must be mad.'

'I probably am. I know it's too soon, but I can't help myself.' His head went back. He looked bleak, uncertain, vulnerable. 'Maggie, my darling, my little love, give me a chance. Make our engagement a real one, and let me start courting you properly, just as I'd intended to do before Alcott and his fellow vultures got to us and pushed me into a corner.'

'You don't know what you're saying...'

'Sweetheart, I do. I love you, Maggie, and I want to spend the rest of my life making you happy. Let me try at least to make you care about me. I know your career means a hell of a lot to you, and you're not interested in marriage—heaven knows you've told me so often enough—but you could combine the two. Other women do it.'

He stood up, kicking the chair away. 'When I saw you walking away from me that day, it was like tearing my heart out. But I had to let you go. I couldn't go on sharing that room night after night, suffering the tortures of the damned, and not have you.'

'But you turned me down.' The words were difficult to say. 'I—asked you—and you...'

'Because I wanted you too much. I knew if I took you, it had to be for life. Marriage or nothing. I didn't think you wanted that.' He gestured impatiently. 'All you ever talked about was breaking off our engagement—never seeing me again. I couldn't face the thought of having you at last—and losing you.'

He sighed. 'And you kept pushing me at Kylie too.' He gave her an accusing glare. 'You seemed to want me to have an affair with her.'

'You didn't seem to mind. You spent enough time with her.'

'I was a guest in her house, for goodness' sake. And she's attractive and amusing—when she's not being a dragon lady.' He whistled appreciatively. 'If she and Gloria Ebelstein ever fall out, it'll be the clash of the Titans all over again. I thought if I hung round her, you might get jealous. But it didn't happen. I couldn't get near you. Every night when I came back to the room, I used to stand and look at you, pretending to be asleep, and I'd ask myself, ''What would she do if I kissed her—took her in my arms?''.' He grimaced. 'Then I'd remember that I'd given you my word I wouldn't start anything, and I'd get into my own bed, and pretend to be asleep too.'

She said in a low voice, 'I—pushed you away, because I felt the same as you—that it had to be all or nothing. I've loved you—wanted to give myself to you—almost from the first, I think, but I was terrified of being a one-night stand—one of a crowd. I dared not take the risk.'

He looked at her gravely, 'Even when you thought I was a rapist?'

'I didn't think that for very long.' Maggie bent her head. 'After all, you supplied me with plenty of evidence about your self-control, from that first night onwards.'

'I was such a bastard to you.' His mouth twisted. 'To be honest, my love, I didn't know what to make of you. You were the first woman I'd met in years who made it clear she'd rather stamp all over my feet than throw herself at them. So I—over-reacted.

'But after I pulled you out of that car, everything changed. I was determined to make you trust me, although I wasn't sure why.' He shuddered. 'I even mended your bloody roof for you—the first time I'd been more than a few feet off the ground in a long time.'

'You're really frightened of heights?' Maggie shook her head. 'I—I thought you were kidding me.'

'No.' His mouth tightened. 'During the pilot for McGuire, the guy doing my stunts was an old friend. I'd actually got him the job. He had a bad fall, and ended up paralysed. He died a year ago.' He gave her a level glance. 'You're not the only one to have nightmares, lady.'

'I'm sorry.'

'Don't be. Going up on that roof was good for me. It was something I needed to face.' He smiled at her, and touched her cheek with his fingertip. 'When you turned to me after your own nightmare, I thought I'd cracked it. That I'd got you to trust me at last. I wanted so badly to hold you, and kiss away everything that had ever hurt or frightened you.

'Then the Press found us, and it all went wrong. I thought I'd lost you, and I was nearly desperate. I started to hope again when you told me about your stepfather at the villa. I told myself you wouldn't have confided in me like that, if you hadn't cared for me a little. But afterwards, I was out in the cold again.'

She flushed. 'I wasn't very cold—that last afternoon.'

'No,' he said gently. 'You were everything I'd dreamed you'd be, my darling. But being able to arouse you sexually is only part of it. Getting you to love me, live with me, fight with me, have my children and grow old with me is something else again.' He took both her hands in his. 'But nothing less will do. Marry me, Maggie. Be my wife.'

'Yes,' she said wonderingly. She looked into his eyes, her face transfigured. 'Oh, darling, yes.'

He looked at her for a long moment, then pulled her into his arms, kissing her deeply, hungrily.

When she could breathe, and speak, she said, 'Jay—I used the spare room again tonight, because I couldn't face the loneliness of the big bed without you. If I—make the running a second time, will you turn me down again?'

He smiled into her hair. 'Try me.'

She looked up at him shyly. 'Darling—I want you so much. Sleep with me, please.'

He laughed, and lifted her off her feet into his arms, holding her against his heart.

'I thought you'd never ask,' he said. And carried her up the stairs into the friendly darkness.

Harlequin Presents®

Coming Next Month

REBECCA YORK

Labeled a "true master of intrigue" by *Rave Reviews*, best-selling author Rebecca York makes her Harlequin Intrigue debut with an exciting suspenseful new series.

It looks like a charming old building near the renovated Baltimore waterfront, but inside 43 Light Street lurks danger . . . and romance.

Let Rebecca York introduce you to:

> *Abby Franklin*—a psychologist who risks everything to save a tough adventurer determined to find the truth about his sister's death. . . .
>
> *Jo O'Malley*—a private detective who finds herself matching wits with a serial killer who makes her his next target. . . .
>
> *Laura Roswell*—a lawyer whose inherited share in a development deal lands her in the middle of a murder. And she's the chief suspect. . . .

These are just a few of the occupants of 43 Light Street you'll meet in Harlequin Intrigue's new ongoing series. Don't miss any of the 43 LIGHT STREET books, beginning with #143 LIFE LINE.

And watch for future LIGHT STREET titles, including #155 SHATTERED VOWS (February 1991) and #167 WHISPERS IN THE NIGHT (August 1991).

HI-143-1